I0822368

The Caddell Project

E.M. Daniels

Book Cover by Andrew Gherman

Illustrations by E.M. Daniels

For those whose inner battles eclipse even the greatest tragedy that may unfold beyond.

Chapter One

Some Day Before, One Day Ahead

Sitting on my bed nearly five miles beneath the Earth, it's painful to remember what life was like up there. An unorganized orchestra of vehicles traveling along busy streets still echoes in the back of my mind. The once-blissful phantom scents of hot dogs rotating on a rack, where the friendly vendor used to sell them every Monday afternoon, now haunt me with nostalgia. To this day, I can still see the lights twinkling against the darkness, silhouettes of massive buildings reaching up to touch the New York City sky. Memories of the world above feel like a searing knife in my chest. I want more than anything to be there, to see it all again. There's so much I didn't get to see.

So much I will *never* get to see.

For everyone else, the Earth has carried on just as we left it. But for the ninety-four of us stuck here, our lives have never been the same. Nothing has been the same since March 5th, 2047. Everything changed that day, especially me.

I was jolted awake early that morning by the sound of glass shattering against the kitchen counter of our apartment. Soon after, I heard screaming and a variety of harsh words, all of which I had been strictly taught never to repeat as a 12-year-old boy. Mom was crying, and Dad wouldn't stop pressing on. Venom was flooding his mouth, spitting out phrases I had never imagined he would say to her.

"It's all ending, Shay, all of it!" he yelled so loud I could feel the vibration in my chest as I sat straight up in bed.

Throwing off my sheets, I didn't even notice the charcoal drawing I had been working on late the night prior flying off my comforter and onto the thick gray carpet. I quickly made my way off the bed, immediately feeling my big toe meet the paper. I sighed with some disappointment as the detailed spaceship lines blurred across the page.

I had spent hours on that sketch. At the time, I believed it was my best work. I remember taking a dozen reference photos from when I snuck into Dad's office and found the model ship displayed on his shelf. I knew he would kill me if he ever found out I had gone in there.

I so badly wanted to pick up my masterpiece and try to fix it, but the commotion coming from the other room took priority. I tiptoed to my cracked door, leaving the smudged drawing on the ground. With caution, I prowled my way into the kitchen.

"See what you've done? Now James knows. Now the world will know, and we can't have that happen, Shay! We can't!" His tone was stern and dire, with tension spreading in the air like an evening fog.

"Do you know what will happen if anyone, absolutely anyone, finds out what is going on?" He slammed his fist into the wooden dining table as his face flushed red with fury.

I winced, jumping at the sound. My eyes started pouring, tears rolling down my cheeks. I was in a pure state of shock. I couldn't move or speak.

"I need to leave. I need to go! I need to get out of here right now, Anthony!" my mom's voice broke in a high-pitched tone.

She left her spot in the corner of the room and stomped towards the doorway, throwing it open as my dad demanded her to stop and come back. He acted like an animal. Never in my life had I seen him like this—never this insane.

I stood frozen at the kitchen doorway, staring at the entrance to our home. There, my mom stood in clear sight of me. As much as I wanted to stop her from walking out the door, I said nothing. She turned back and looked at me. I remember it clear as day. Her eyes were filled with sadness that radiated within her. Yet, when she saw my gaze find hers for the last time, I could feel her love for me and our little family seeping through her withered thoughts.

She shut the door and was gone. I stood there for what felt like hours—though it was only a few minutes—waiting for her to come back inside. But for whatever reason, something far greater than anything I'd ever known made her drive away.

I turned to see Dad sitting empty at the kitchen table. As I did, he instantly turned his head towards me, sensing my eyes on him as I stood motionless. My mind held a tight grasp on my lungs as I stared blankly. I felt like I couldn't breathe.

He stood up and walked over to me. I was always tall for my age, and although I was young, my eyes met directly with his as he approached. I saw hate and sorrow, so much pain filling him. I looked closely, searching for the man who had cared for me my entire life. I searched for my father as I stared into the maze of his eyes, but the old him was nowhere to be found.

No matter how hard I tried, he wasn't there.

The next moment, I was faced with the pounding pain I felt as he struck me. He came in from the left side of my face, knocking me to the ground. I thought many things were scary growing up, but nothing compared to the fear I felt at that very moment.

He kept punching me. Soon after, I felt it in my left shoulder, then my right arm. He kicked my shin before grabbing me violently by my shirt, lifting me off the floor, and slamming me into the wall. I saw red, so much red. After that, everything went black.

I woke up what seemed like days later, somehow ending up in the passenger seat of my father's car. Through a daze, my first instinct was to pull down the overhead mirror and look at myself. The image in that reflection is one I will never be able to erase. Staring back at me were two black eyes, a split lip, and dried blood firmly engraved into my right eyebrow.

As I closed the mirror, I realized I couldn't look quickly in any specific direction without my vision spinning. I turned to him slowly as he stared forward. Building up the strength to say anything felt like trying to lift a semi off the ground with two fingers. I just kept looking at him, and eventually, he broke the silence for me.

"You see, everything is going to end, James." The words were merely a whisper coming from his dried lips. I don't think I even blinked as he began talking.

"The others and I have discovered a sort of... rip or tear. I guess that's the best way to say it." He reached up his hand and wiped it once over his face, dragging down his bottom eyelids before proceeding. "On November 23rd of 2052, this 'tear' in Earth's atmosphere will become a hole, and once it does..." His voice trailed off as he thought. I could do nothing but hold onto his every word.

"This hole will cause what we have referred to as 'The Ripple.' This is an event in which the pressure caused by the space around us will make the entire surface of Earth lift and pull in that area." He paused for just a moment, briefly mumbling to himself before proceeding.

"From there, it will send a wave around the planet, causing a ripple across the entire surface." Water began to form in his eyes again, though he never broke his vision from the road ahead.

"Everything will be destroyed. Everything still up here will turn to dust, and life will no longer be able to exist." I watched as his bottom lip shook. A part of me wanted to feel bad for him, a part of me wanted to jump out of this car onto the highway, and another part of me still needed to know more.

I looked at the road in front of us. None of this was real. How could this be real? I sat there, my mouth gaping open. My body hurt too much to cry.

"I need you to understand what we are doing now, okay?" He swiped across his wet cheeks and put both of his arms on the top of the steering wheel. My body began shaking as I attempted to listen to his concentrated tone.

I thought I had died that day. This man, who always claimed my love, had beaten me nearly to death, yet he was still trying to reason with me. I was too weak to argue against him.

"Soon, we will be at a place that I have been building. A place where you, me, and some others are chosen to be from now on for as long as we live." His voice radiated through me. As much as it hurt, I couldn't help but sit forward just a tad more. I sat in silence and held my breath as he continued, picking up on the slight change in his hopeless tone.

"You are one of what we call 'The Selected.' Soon, you will officially begin your time serving humanity in 'The Caddell Project.'"

At that moment, he finally turned his head toward me. His eyes again met mine before turning back to the asphalt before us. I knew Dad had been working on a secret project for a long time, but I never could have expected it to be this severe. It felt so different hearing our last name used in such a daunting way.

Pure silence drifted between us for miles as we left the highway. We drove through paths of unknown territory before entering a coded gate surrounded by a chain-link fence. Once inside, we parked at the secured entrance that only a few others in the world had ever seen.

An entrance that led to the depths of my father's creation.

"Here, you are just James. You can't tell anyone that you are a Caddell. Do you understand me?" I just stared at him with hazed eyes. My body ached and throbbed with every breath. I said nothing in return, not just because of the pain, but because of the overwhelming railroads of emotions and thoughts blazing in every direction inside of me.

"I said, do you understand?" He slammed his hand on the steering wheel.

As the always-obedient kid I had grown to be, I nodded once in return, my head pounding with the motion. So much of me wanted him to hit me again. I wanted him to look me in the eyes when he did it so he could see my pain.

His pain.

My head felt heavier after the downward motion, and my vision fell away once again as the darkness washed over me. At that time, I don't remember any more of our conversation or how we actually got down here. All I remember was waking up, gasping for air as the same man hovered over my limp body on a cold table.

The panic attack quickly faded as I inhaled the oxygen—the one thing keeping us all alive every second. If only I had known then that as I wore an oxygen mask in those few waking moments, it would soon become the very item I got most familiar with.

I recall the bright lights and my father's voice ringing through me as he cried, clinging tightly to my hand. Why would he cry when he was the one who did this to me? He caused me this much hurt, just to save my life in front of a room full of people I had never met.

Maybe one day, I will finally get my answer.

He held my back straight as I sat up and life came to me again. I felt like I was in a totally different world—like somehow it was just a dream. I leisurely observed my surroundings, noting every detail. The room was concrete, and it was so cold. It also looked as though it was definitely designed for medical purposes. There was a sink in the corner along with bins of first-aid items stacked against every wall.

Through all the people that surrounded me as I awoke, one individual specifically caught my attention. She stood firmly in the back against the wall and appeared to be around my age, from what I could see. Her light brown hair glimmered in the overhead light. A smile began to wash over her worried expression as I looked in her direction.

It wasn't long before her crossed arms unraveled and a gentle wave of her hand was sent my way. Little did I know that while my father had been the one to stop me from dying, she would be the real one to save me.

The last specific moment I remember clearly from that day was the words she told me when she eventually parted the crowd of people and came over to my dreary self sitting on that table.

"Welcome home," she said in a near whisper, her echoed voice still bouncing within me all these years later.

It had been the first time she had referred to Caddell as home, the first time anyone had called this place anything close to a home.

Now, tomorrow is November 23rd, and Caddell will become our only home.

The only place left on the entire planet to call home.

Chapter Two

The Sketch and The Suit

Snap! My pencil lead breaks just as I'm in the middle of sketching an important drawing of my pet fish in the corner of my nightstand. I study him, ensuring I capture every little detail of his shimmering scales. Leaning closer, I watch as he swims so peacefully, admiring what it must be like to spend all day in a calm and comforting space like he does.

"You know, Zoron, sometimes I envy you. You don't have to worry about testing days or impending apocalypses," I muse, tapping lightly on the glass of the tank.

I feel the edge of my mouth curve upward, a smile forming as I observe him. It doesn't take more than a few seconds for my attention to dwindle, and I soon find myself staring at my reflection in the clear glass of his tank.

My hazel eyes look back at me, and I admire my features for a brief moment. The mask suctioned tightly to my skin constantly distorts the lower half of my face. Honestly, sometimes I even forget what I look like. It's been years since I've seen James Caddell, both mentally and physically.

My dark, wavy hair falls effortlessly, sculpting the edges of my face with a soft curl flowing above my right eye. Briskly, I use my fingers as a comb to adjust the loose hair until it thoroughly covers the scar beneath. It's as if I'm trying to hide it before anyone else sees it, yet I'm the only person in the room.

I shake my head, and instantly, the hint of a smile beneath my eyes fades. I never smile, truthfully, because there's really nothing left for me to smile about.

Well, almost nothing.

Just as I'm about to grab a new pencil to finish my sketch and continue my conversation with Zoron, the door bursts open. There, her silhouette leans against the doorframe. I scramble to hide my slight embarrassment, hastily grabbing a book from my cluttered desk and pretending to be engrossed in its contents.

It is, of course, the one and only Jess Mercer. My best friend since the day this all started. She stands with her leg propped slightly to the side, her arms crossed casually. Glancing up quickly, back and forth from my book, I see her raise an eyebrow. Per usual, she is unimpressed by my charade.

"What are you doing, James?" Jess asks, tilting her head knowingly as she leans against the doorframe.

"Just... reading," I reply sheepishly. I feel my cheeks flush as I try to maintain a concentrated expression. I just hope my mask is hiding every bit of pink pigment I can feel growing on my face.

"You know, if you keep pretending to read, you might actually learn something," she teases, her hair catching the light overhead as she winks at me.

I chuckle nervously and scratch the back of my head. "Yeah, yeah, I'll add it to my to-do list," I say, fully aware that I won't. I roll my eyes, knowing full well Jess is right. I am notorious for my punctuality, or lack thereof, and today is no exception.

Jess shakes her head and turns back around. "You're lucky we're friends. Hurry up, idiot, or you'll be late again." She leaves the door cracked slightly open as she goes.

I grab my drawstring bag off the ground and toss my sketchpad into it along with a handful of pencils from my desk. Quickly, I throw myself around the room, over to my dresser of messy drawers against the wall. I rummage through until I find my favorite black leather combat boots and fumble while struggling far more than I should to get them onto my feet. By the second boot, I'm too lazy to tie it properly, so tucking the ends of the laces into the tight edges above my ankle seems like a better solution.

Jumping back up, I proceed to study myself in the full-body mirror stashed in the corner. I stand still, breathing rapidly as the suit shifts against my body. The oxygen plates and mask fasten over my mouth, with tubes leading down to my chest, supplying me every second with the air I need to survive.

As I stand there admiring my posture in the green metallic suit, I can't help but marvel at its design. The material feels smooth and surprisingly light, hugging my body like a second skin. The reflective surface glints under the artificial lights, giving off a scaly, textured sheen. This is no ordinary suit, it's a living machine created through hours of pure dedication by my father.

The design is sleek, with streamlined seams and integrated panels that allow for maximum flexibility and movement. It is tailored to fit the human form perfectly, with articulated joints that move with my body effortlessly. As I sway, the suit adjusts to my every motion, the surface appearing as a kaleidoscope of green hues. It's like wearing a real, living partner that provides nourishment and life support.

Tiny, microscopic channels run throughout the fabric, enabling it to capture sunlight and convert it into energy, just like a plant. I can feel a gentle warmth spreading across my skin as the suit begins its photosynthesis process, drawing in the sunlight-mimicking structures attached to the ceilings of every room and converting it into vital nutrients.

Beneath the outer layer, the suit is lined with a network of synthetic fibers designed to absorb carbon dioxide and release oxygen. I take a deep breath, feeling the pure, fresh air fill my lungs. The suit is doing the breathing for me, recycling the air and ensuring I always have a supply of clean oxygen.

I am not a fit-bodied individual, more of a tall and thin boy with the only muscle definition I have somehow being in my buttocks. Instinctively, I turn to the side and tilt my head back, clenching my muscles and standing with one leg farther forward than the other.

"Trying out for a superhero pose, or just admiring your best asset?" she startles me with her voice from the doorway.

"Hey, I thought you left!" I jump, snatching my bag of supplies off the floor in front of me like a shield as an instant reaction. "Why are you still here...?" I trail off while my mind wanders for something to say in the seconds that pass, trying to hide my slight insecurity.

"Do you like the view or something?" Mentally, I can't help but applaud myself for that one.

"I was just going to tell you to make sure you bring your glow torch, just in case today. Oh, you would love me to say yes to that one, wouldn't you? In your dreams, pretty boy." She shuts the door completely this time, and I hear her footsteps heading down the hall.

I nearly eat the ground, tripping over my untucked shoelace as I stretch toward the door. Hurriedly, I finish tying the untrustworthy boot and resume my task of reaching for the handle. I open it, and it flies so hard I don't have a chance to catch it before the metal pings loudly as it hits the wall behind it. Grabbing the doorframe and swinging my arm to meet contact with the handle once again, I pull the door rapidly behind me as I chase after her down the hall.

Attempting the smooth move I intend to make, I make my way in front of her down the long concrete hallway before we enter the meeting room. I have to prove a point here—if she wants to be picky about me being late, then I might as well be earlier than her at least. Once ahead, I turn my head over my shoulder, flashing her a quick wink with a slight trace of a smile before turning into the room buzzing with people.

Like I said before, I don't have much of a reason to smile. When I do, I don't really know if anyone ever sees my efforts. Maybe it's because they don't give me a chance to smile back, or maybe they're too busy looking past me to ever see it in the first place. Either way, none of that really matters. I have everything I need right here. I still have my one reason to smile, even if it is the last reason I have left.

I have Jess.

Chapter Three

The Color Red

"Please, take a seat, everyone," the head scientist's voice echoes through the massive underground meeting room. For me, it isn't the same as it is for the others, something similar to getting a lecture from their teacher. Instead, I am forced to pretend that I am just like them when I am not. He isn't my teacher or just a scientist. He is my father, yet no one can know that.

I don't want to admit it, but there is no denying the facts. He is a handsome man who holds himself in the most appropriate posture. His hair has an array of soft curls similar to my own, but with a lighter pigment. He is strong and tall, with a tight curve about his jawline. To be as evil as I know he truly is, he has diamonds for eyes. The beaming lights above capture the silhouette of each person within the metal room, taking us in through what he sees and reflecting out what is left.

As I timidly step into the meeting room, the weight of everyone's gaze bears down on me like an oppressive force. Each pair of eyes seems to carry its own judgment, amplifying the already thick tension hanging in the air. My late arrival only intensifies the situation, leaving me exposed to face every expression directed my way.

Attempting to blend into the background, I slip into the room with as little disturbance as possible, hoping to escape notice. However, fate has different intentions as Jess follows closely behind me, her presence somehow rendering her immune to the embarrassment.

"Ah, James, so glad you could join us."

His voice shatters the silence, its sharpness slicing through the atmosphere with precision. It rings out, a contrast to the hushed murmurs that surround it. The words pierce through me, igniting a wave of embarrassment that floods my cheeks with heat. As I sink into my seat, I can't shake the feeling of being under a magnifying glass, every imperfection laid bare for everyone to see.

"As you all know, tomorrow is the day we have been anticipating for the past several years." His strong voice echoes through the chamber. We all sit in a massive underground room; even the smallest pencil falling to the floor makes echoes bounce from every wall.

The room is colossal, easily the size of a football field, with ceilings that arch so high they seem to vanish into shadows. Rows of metal benches stretch out in perfectly aligned formations, bolted to the polished concrete floor. The walls, lined with reinforced steel, loom like silent sentinels, their cold surfaces reflecting the bright lights that hang from above. These lights cast long, eerie shadows that flicker and dance with every movement.

Despite its size, the room feels oppressive, as if the weight of the world above is pressing down on us. The air is cool and dry, with a faint metallic scent that clings to everything, even through the high-level filtration of the masks we wear. High above, a network of pipes crisscrosses, barely visible but ever-present, hinting at the complex infrastructure that keeps this place running.

Jess and I exchange playful banter from across the room, our regular antics penetrating the gravity of the situation at hand. We always have to listen to the same repetitive spiel we've heard countless times before about the impending event known as "The Ripple," the phenomenon that will tear a hole in the atmosphere, unleashing a devastating wave of pressure that will annihilate all life on the surface of the Earth. Yes, we understand that part already.

My father flips the page at his podium at the front of the room. "The Ripple will occur at exactly 8:03 a.m. on November 23rd. Tomorrow, anything and everything living on Earth's surface will be destroyed in a time span shorter than the blink of an eye. Nothing will be left; everything will turn to dust. Everything except those of you in this very room."

Jess makes that same face she always does when she's disappointed in something I'm doing. Her eyebrows are knitted together, her forehead making one horizontal line in the center. Classic Jess. I lean back in my chair, trying to disappear behind the nervous boy sitting next to me. Maybe if I blend into the background, she'll forget I'm here and won't pay attention to me if I mess with him some. Yeah, right.

Peeking over the boy's shoulder, I can see Jess's expression hasn't softened one bit. She's like a hawk, eyes locked on me, her silent judgment piercing through the classroom noise. I stifle a sigh and decide to respond in my usual mature way: rolling my eyes dramatically.

The boy beside me is tapping his pencil on the desk in a relentless, rhythmic pattern. It's like he's trying to send a Morse code message to aliens or something. I start mimicking his anxious taps, matching his rhythm exactly. For a second, it's almost like we're in sync, communicating through this weird, shared beat. Then I push my luck, adding a little flourish to the rhythm, and before I know it, I slip up and let out a laugh.

The boy turns, glaring at me with wide, anxious eyes. He looks like a startled deer caught in headlights. His stare is both accusing and bewildered. "What's your problem?" his eyes seem to say.

I quickly straighten up, my laughter dying in my throat. Jess's glare has now transformed into full-on exasperation, and the boy's glare is starting to burn a hole through my forehead. I can feel my face heating up, and I sink lower into my seat, mumbling an apology.

"Sorry," I mutter, trying to suppress a grin. The boy huffs and goes back to his tapping, though he proceeds a bit more cautiously now, like he's afraid I might join in again. Jess, on the other hand, shakes her head slowly. Probably wondering how she ended up with someone like me as a friend.

"James," a voice speaks firmly. I turn quickly in my chair to face the eyes of the one who owns us all. "Is this a joke to you?"

"No, sir. Sorry, sir. It won't happen again, sir," I stumble, holding back the devious smirk in my eyes.

"That's what I thought. Now, as I was saying..." he proceeds.

"Your oxygen masks are made to last you a lifetime. Don't break them, and don't remove them for anything. Understood?" He keeps going on and on about the safety precautions we've heard a dozen times. I just rely on Jess to fill me in on anything particularly life-threatening I should know about.

I wasn't taught in school like most people. Instead, my learning has come strictly from my own experiences and the scientific principles my father instilled in me. I used to think often about what it would have been like to learn in school. Maybe if I had, I wouldn't struggle as much as I do. Though, I've ultimately concluded that there's no easy way to fix me, regardless of exactly how I acquire knowledge. After all, there's no textbook that teaches you how to survive a mental illness and a global apocalypse at the same time.

Rather than getting harassed again by the overpowering voice in the room, I decide to pull out my sketchbook and start creating a physical copy of my thoughts. Taking out my lovely charcoal pencil, I begin scribbling away. I continue to add details as I sketch, blending the lines softly with my fingertips as he keeps speaking.

"Embrace today as your last day, your final day walking the halls of your familiar home chambers. Prepare for your tasks, and rest well. I know each of you are ready."

The meeting is a blur of instructions and last-minute preparations, and I struggle to focus as my mind races with thoughts of what lies ahead. Jess gets up with the rest of the crowd to head back and prepare for the day to come. I tell her to go on without me. I am immersed in my continuous lines and shades, using them to express my emotions.

As the session draws to a close, I find myself face-to-face with him, alone in the vast room, his stern figure exuding disapproval that hangs heavy in the air.

"James," my father begins as he approaches me, his voice low and authoritative.

In front of me, the pencil in my hand never stops. The details are starting to come together. I am grasping onto my oxygen plates attached to my chest while my father's shadow looms over me. A dark charcoal outline interprets the darkness inside him. My drawing conveys the pain in my chest as he is always there and never even cares. I like to draw everything I do from my own perspective as a way to physically see the emotions I'm feeling in a moment.

"James, are you listening?"

I quickly slam my sketchbook shut before he gets close enough to see it.

"You know how important tomorrow is. We can't afford any mistakes."

I nod, my jaw tightening with frustration as he keeps going.

"That girl. I don't want you getting any closer to her, James. Do you understand me?" he forces into me.

My eyes leave the cover of my book and glare up at him.

"You mean Jess? She's my best friend, if you even bothered to care enough to realize that." I continue, saying more than I should. "She means more to me than you ever will."

I know he's going to hit me before he even starts to lift his arm. He shoves me hard on my left shoulder—the same one that stayed bruised when I was a kid.

"You will always respect me, James. No matter what, you will never tell her who you really are! Do you understand me now?"

I clench my teeth and flare my nostrils. It takes everything, every single part of me not to fight back. I am bigger now, and I know I could hurt him if I tried. Here, though, I am just James. I am not a Caddell. I am not a fighter, either. He can hit me forever, and I am never going to touch him. I know I have to be superior to his ways.

Little does he know that Jess already knows.

"Yes... sir," I grunt.

"Good. Now get up and head to bed. Big day tomorrow."

He shoves the back of my head hard as he walks sternly out of the room. I try to catch myself before my nose makes contact with my sketchbook, but it slams against the cover anyway. A thick red liquid begins to pour from both sides, bubbling upward and filling the top edges of my oxygen mask. The built-in cleaning function cleanses the edges of my nostrils as I sniffle.

I tell myself he will change, but I know he never will. Here I am, once again broken by the end of the night, and yet I still go on. He just can't stop, and I will never be able to understand why. I still sit here like I always do, just begging for more.

I groan and hit my palm flat against the table. Then the coughing fit starts as the filtration system keeps flushing the substance over the top and out of the sides without sacrificing my air quality.

To Jess and the others here, I play a game of pretending, trying to be the seventeen-year-old boy that I am. I'm not supposed to cry, but sometimes, when a boy is alone in the dark, it becomes the best time to break.

I'm tired of the constant pressure, tired of living in the void of expectations I can never seem to meet. I feel like a shadow. I'm right there in front of everyone, yet they always walk straight through me. I'm ready, ready for it all to be over and this torture to end. But it's never going to. Sometimes I question my own existence, like maybe I did die all those years ago.

Or maybe sometimes I just wish that I did.

I sit by myself in the silent room until, eventually, I've had enough for now. The blood on my face has dried, along with my watering eyes. I stand, rubbing my eyes to adjust my vision, and gather my soaked sketchbook to head back to my chamber.

I find myself trapped in my thoughts once again after I drop my items on the floor and make my way to bed. As always, I fall into a familiar spiral. My mind drifts back to the day it all began. I lie here, just breathing, as each passing day I slowly forget what it's like to actually live. Sinking deeper into the recesses of the memories, I still wonder if I will ever be free from the burden of my past.

"Hey, stranger, what happened this time?" Her elegant voice penetrates the dark tunnel in my mind.

Jess makes her way into the room. Usually, she makes some form of a loud entrance, but this time, she comes in calmly and sits on the end of my bed. Her amber-brown eyes show me glimpses of sympathy as she turns her face toward mine, her legs still dangling off the edge.

I scoot up out of my covers, revealing the blood-coated edges of my nose that run down the tubes tracing my neck. I watch as she tries to contain herself from reacting to the pain she knows I'm in.

"I mean, red is definitely your color." She turns her worried look into a glimpse of hope. Somehow, through everything, she always knows how to be happy. She always can make me happy when I never feel as though I can be.

"Thanks, Jessica. I think a bloody nose is a new trend myself. I most certainly had him slam my head into the table on purpose. Nice touch, don't you think?" I focus every ounce of my attention on her, grinning with the edges of my worn eyes. She swats her hand at my leg; she always hates it when I call her Jessica.

"Okay, sir, I came in here to check on you, but I'm not going to stay if you're going to be an idiot, JJ."

She gave me that nickname the day I was brought to this hole in the ground. It's short for the lovely name "Just James," as the man who can't call me his son says. I know Jess and I would never be able to separate after the day we first met, whether that means we'll always be friends or maybe one day something more.

"You know you're my favorite, right?" I want to say so much more to her, but the guard that grows inside always stops me from telling her.

"Of course I am!" She spits back at me and gets up off the bed. "Now I'm going to head back and get some sleep alone in my comfy chamber for the last time, okay? Go clean your face and get some rest, too, for me. I don't want to deal with cranky JJ along with everyone else tomorrow."

"Roger that, Jessica." I remark, feeling the tension between us growing every time we get to spend little moments like this together. She giggles to herself and makes her way out of the room, shutting the door carefully behind her in an attempt not to be seen near me at such hours.

She is right about what she said. This is our last time like this. This is our final night being alone and not having to live by the stern rules in Caddell. Being in the never-ending presence of my father truly makes me want out of here more than anything. If I'm being honest, most days I wish I were one of the billions left on the surface tomorrow, rather than being contained down here with him.

My mind still needs to be free to ever be at peace. That is, of course, if peace even exists at all in the first place. Staring blankly at the wall, the thought of sleeping doesn't even cross my mind, and counting sheep is impossible when you don't remember fully what sheep even look like anymore. My nose still throbs, and the building weight of the people and the world around me is consuming me. I wish I could have a moment just to myself, some time away from this prison.

I need an escape.

Chapter Four

Vivi armis

That's it! That's what I need! I sit up quickly. This is my last day, my final day of ever being completely alone in this everlasting trap of a foreign realm. Jess's words spark an entirely new door of thoughts within me. This really is our last night before we will all have to live in Caddell together. People aren't really my strong suit, and honestly, if none of them existed but Jess, I think I would prefer it that way. I may be just James to them, but this James knows things that others never will. I can get into Caddell myself, where others can't. Which also means I can go experience the world alone for the first time, and the last.

Jumping out of bed, I wipe myself off the best I can with my bed covers. The sheets stick to my skin like a second layer as I do so. I wince, peeling them off like a bandage from a wound. My fingers trace the edges of my oxygen mask, feeling the familiar texture of dried blood I've become accustomed to, and begin checking each part of my oxygen system.

Standing in the mirror, I make triple sure that I still have all three tubes connected thoroughly to the rectangular, gray-colored plates attached to my chest. From there, I follow them to their respective areas on my face mask. I tuck both sides behind my ears and ensure that it fits securely under my chin and over my nose and mouth.

It looks neat and clean, like a surgical mask a doctor would wear, only this one is much cooler. It is metallic-colored with a shiny hue and reflects even the slightest amount of light. In fine engraved print in the right corner near my jawline, the words "Vivi armis" are clearly visible. It is one of my favorite concepts my father ever thought of. It quite literally translates from Latin to "living armor" in English.

It has the ability to transform the components of carbon dioxide into oxygen. Caddell's biggest downfall is that it primarily only consists of carbon dioxide; there is no oxygen supply able to be added to its natural air quality. Pressing the button of my mask on the backside of my right ear, the edges of the material suction tightly to my face, ensuring no outside air can travel in or out. I fix my hair around my eyes and look back at myself, my eyes showing all of my emotion without the lower half of my face visible.

"Stop looking at yourself, James," I mumble to myself before reaching down and grabbing my bag with a few items still left in it. I added my sketchpad again just in case and would have brought my one extra oxygen tube if it weren't broken, which I never told Dad about.

In order for this to work, I make sure to take off my embedded shoulder tracker and place it neatly under my covers. This way, no alarms will sound, and everyone's beloved James will appear to be sleeping the night away in his bed.

I toss my bag over my shoulder, still making sure my suit is completely secured before creaking open the door. I'm about to step into the hallway when I realize I nearly forgot my glow torch. I skip back inside and snatch it quickly off my nightstand. Slipping through my door and closing it quietly behind me, I scan the hall briefly before proceeding. It's 4:00 a.m. anyway; there's no way anyone is up at this hour.

Silently and swiftly, I navigate the labyrinthine corridors, each turn a calculated step closer to my destination. The echo of my footsteps reverberates, a contrast to the silence that envelops the clandestine passages. Shadows dance on the walls, casting eerie shapes that seem to whisper secrets of their own.

I turn a sharp corner, only to find myself paused in front of the door to Jess's room. For a moment, I consider turning back around. I'm sure she's still asleep, lying on her side with her legs tucked close to her torso. Another part of me wants to crack open the door and persuade her to come with me, but the larger half of me insists I go alone.

I inhale and keep going through with my original mission. I can almost feel the weight of my father's expectations pressing down on me, his teachings echoing in my mind with each step. "Patience, precision, perseverance," he'd say. For some, hearing their father's voice would be comforting, but for me, it's closer to haunting.

By the age of fourteen, I had committed each combination to memory, a skill learned through delicate observation without him even knowing. Every subtle movement, every calculated pause, had been buried into my mind. Tonight, it was my turn to put those skills to the test.

The first door has a brass keypad worn smooth from years of use. I approach it with cautious confidence, my fingers grazing over the familiar sequence. A quiet beep signals my success, and the lock disengages with a soft ting. The door creaks open, and I slip through, ensuring it closes silently behind me.

Beyond it, the second door looms, newer and more sophisticated. Its sleek, electronic sealing system glows faintly in the dim light. I pause for a moment, recalling the swift, fluid motions my father uses. With a deep breath, I enter the next code, the mechanical vibrations of the door sliding open echoing faintly in the narrow passageway. I glance over my shoulder, the shadows playing tricks on my mind, before pressing forward.

The third barrier is the most daunting, a fusion of old and new security technologies. It requires not only a code but also a precise series of pressure points on the door's surface. My heart pounds as I position my hand, my fingertips dancing across the cool metal. I count silently, pressing each point in the exact order I have memorized. When the final point clicks into place, the door shudders and unlocks. I exhale a breath I didn't realize I'd been holding and nudge the door open just enough to slip through.

Finally, the fourth door. My father always lingers at this door, as if contemplating something greater before opening. The code here is the most complex: 2-6-8-4-6-6-9-5-4-3-7. As I key it in, I feel a surge of adrenaline, each faint tap bringing me closer to my goal.

The lock disengages with a satisfying thud, and the door swings open.

Ahead lies the threshold to a new world, its entrance marked by the familiar etchings and imposing stature that I have come to know so well. As I approach, the intricate details of its construction come into focus, each groove and hinge created with precision. Reaching into my bag, I pull out my glow torch and, instantly, the warm glow casts a silver reflection before me, illuminating the name of the project as a constant reminder.

In a bold font, the singular word "CADDELL" screams back at me. A name that is mine, yet it belongs now to something much larger than myself. I stand for what seems longer than it actually is, admiring the outside of this entirely new ecosystem secured beyond. This will be the last time I will likely ever be able to see it from this point of view.

I step forward those few more feet between us, closing the gap that separates me from the door into the inner world. Placing my hand on the scanning pad, I watch as it searches its database before a green check mark appears above.

Dad can spend his life trying to convince people that I'm not a Caddell, but he can't change that I will always be one by blood.

Chapter Five

Illumination

The pressure releases as the massive door creaks open. Light from within glows radiantly over me, painting the walls with a blurred silhouette. I tuck my torch back into my drawstring as the new light fills my view. The opening is just big enough for me to slip inside. Swiftly, I sneak in. The massive door makes a loud screech before suctioning shut behind me.

For a moment, I am able to experience this place and explore myself without rules or others around me. Just a few hours left, yet it is all worth it to feel a sense of independence for a change. I can finally understand what it is like to be Zoron, freely wandering within the limits of his own home.

It is a sight unlike any other. No matter how much I hate the idea of being here forever, I can never deny how truly remarkable it is. A hollow world inside the one we all used to know. The entire place is filled with plants, massive ones that grow sideways and turn upside down. They are purple and blue, with every color shimmering over their leaves, which range in size and shape. Each leaf seems to dance to its own rhythm, defying anything ever considered normal above.

Looking up, the sunlight-mimicking lights are so high I can barely see a separation between them. They are the reason we can live here, as they create a near-exact replication of the sun's light and energy. Sunlight is the true key to life, regardless of what those textbooks say. Some people think it's oxygen, and others say it's water. Here, though, we have water, and our chest plates and masks convert the carbon-enriched toxic atmosphere into oxygen for us. The only thing Caddell needs in addition to ourselves is the sun, and my father has devoted his life to ensuring we will have it.

We are all that Earth has left.

In Caddell, time seems to move differently. It's not just the constant hum of the artificial suns, it's a feeling that life somehow goes by just a bit quicker here. Within the surreal flora and the artificial glow, I am constantly reminded of the endless potential of human ingenuity. As much as I may long for the familiarity of the world above, a part of me can't help but be captivated by the wonder Caddell possesses.

The "Center Port House," as we call it, is designed to produce an endless supply of food for us. It uses carbon dioxide, sunlight, and water to create meals through a process similar to photosynthesis in plants. This house has rooms for all of us and is located at the center of Caddell. Our meals contain all the dietary necessities we need in a single serving, and thankfully so, because believe me we don't eat them by choice. It's not the most appealing task. I guess we can't complain too much, though. We're the few left to live at all in the first place.

If I keep going straight from the entrance I just came through and slightly to the right, I will start to see the gravel path that leads to its familiar doors. I've spent enough time preparing for the rest of my life living in that house, though, and right now I want to see something new.

The bright lights above illuminate everything around me as I branch off and make my way to the left. By continuing down a new path, I already start to see things I never even knew existed. The floor appears as though it would be rubbery and squish beneath my feet, yet it leaves nothing but the secure tap of my boots on the oddly solid ground with each step. I can look around forever and see no boundaries. As long as we've been here, there is still so much left unexplored.

As I press forward, the trail seems to grow longer. I step carefully over some strange-looking mushrooms I've never seen before. They are taller than they are round, with sharp triangular points facing in every direction. There are all sorts of strange organisms here, and Jess always teases me for never going anywhere without my boots. Clearly, she's never stepped on anything like these.

I continue to watch every step, soon finding myself quickly approaching a massive, blue, vine-sculpted tunnel. It is long and dimly lit, consisting of twisting, leafy vines wrapped tightly together over the path ahead, forming a narrow way for me to crawl through to the other side.

I bend down and set my drawstring to the side. Leaning closer to the firm flooring, I catch a glimpse of light seeping from the other side. Before entering the unknown, I check the time once again. I have no idea how long the tunnel truly goes or how long it will take to get to the other side. I know I have only two options: either go back and get to my chamber before anyone realizes I'm missing, or go through and explore this tunnel alone before anyone else finds it. I like the second choice better.

I tuck my drawstring close to the edge of the tunnel, where it stays secured until I come back through. I want to take it with me, but there just isn't enough space for us both to fit through. Fixing my posture until I am on my hands and knees, I peel back the vines slightly blocking the opening and make my way inside, instantly being enclosed once again in the dim surroundings once the vine behind me falls back into place.

I cautiously make my way toward the beacon of light in front of me and start to take in the slight glowing edges of the tunnel. As I get further, the little lines woven into the leaves emit neon shades of glowing blue. It isn't enough to allow me to see perfectly clearly, but each individual pattern draws my attention.

The end is growing closer as I pass the center of the tunnel, but I can't help but be fascinated by the dancing light show all around me. Pivoting, I manage to fold myself back into a sitting position. I wish I could have brought my drawstring with me. I totally would have grabbed my sketchbook and just stayed here forever, drawing all of the different shapes.

I reach out my hand and, using my pointer finger, I follow one of the brighter, light-colored blue patterns down, left, and back up again before it disappears and a new section sparks. For the first time in such a long time, I think I am starting to remember what peace feels like again.

I reach my hand out once again to follow the calming glow but instantly jerk backward as I feel a slight tingle through my finger as it touches the surface. Maybe they aren't made for me to touch, but they sure are amazing to watch. I sit there forever, watching the light show as it grows brighter before returning to darkness. I am mesmerized. I don't think I have ever been more entertained by something.

"Shoot!" I say out loud, as if the vines need to hear my disappointment, as I scan the flickering watch on my left wrist.

"You're kidding me." It's already 7:23 a.m. I know for a fact I have not been in here for that long. At least, I don't think I have been. If I'm being honest, I really do completely forget I am supposed to be working for a limited amount of time here. I can't believe there's only about half an hour until everyone comes to join me here, and that also means that there is less than one hour before the surface of Earth is gone.

At this point, I'm sure Jess is already wondering where I am. She's an early riser, of course. I mean, she is Jess after all. She's meticulous and orderly, and I'm, well, let's just say I'm quite the opposite.

I decide it's probably best if I make my way back, though so much of me wants to just stay here as the world above makes its way to the end, and I know I will soon be joined by all the rest of them down here. Moving my sore bottom up off of the firm ground, I start to adjust myself back into a toddler crawling position to make my way back out.

"I have got to show this to Jess when she's here," I say out loud to myself as I stop just one more time to view the weaving colors on all sides of me. My rare smile grows at the thought of getting to show my findings to Jess. Maybe it's my time to tell her everything. Maybe I can finally tell her that I—

"Nee-naw, nee-naw, nee-naw..."

I jump back, startled, as my thoughts are cut short. The ear-piercing sound of emergency alarm sirens starts to ring and echo, bouncing off of the walls and blocking out all other sounds across the entire ecosystem.

My chest plates begin to fire off their own alarm in near sync with the sirens outside as I feel myself begin breathing far too quickly. I scramble around back and forth for a moment before crawling at full speed back in the direction I had come from, now through only memory. We have trained with these sirens before, and even though a part of me at first thinks it might be because I was missing, the pace of the alarm is wrong. This is something else, something much bigger.

The sound pounds through my head and chest with each radiating wave they emit. I try not to panic, but it's no use, of course. I always have fear engraved into my core. With each forward motion, I can feel the skin on my kneecaps scraping as they slam into the hard ground. My wrists and palms ache, but I can barely even feel the pain over my anxiety.

"Ughhh!" I groan in the darkness between the noises around me, pushing on, though my arms and legs are getting weaker with each push.

The ground and walls of the tunnel shake, and I can hear crashing from outside. As I press on, I hear cracking and falling of large things outside, but with my vision impaired, I can't see anything beyond the vines. Even the glow on the walls around me is nothing but a faint blur as I travel. The opening is still so far away, and all I can do to remotely control myself is focus on the shining light that I will soon be greeted with, as long as I keep going. My lungs burn, and my oxygen system is maxed out as I make it work beyond its limits.

As I stand frozen in fear, the ominous sound grows louder, drawing nearer with each passing moment. Then, with a deafening screech, something massive collides with the ground just behind me, shattering the silence into pure chaos. The impact reverberates through the room, sending shockwaves of panic rippling through my body.

I feel the hairs on the back of my neck stand on end as the crashing of the object echoes in my ears, mingling with the sharp symphony of shattered glass. It is as if time has slowed to a crawl, each shard of glass spinning through the air like deadly projectiles, piercing through everything in their path.

Instinct kicks in like a bolt of lightning, propelling me into action with a sense of urgency I've never felt before. My heart races, pounding against my chest like a drumbeat as adrenaline surges through my veins. With a sharp intake of breath, I push myself forward, my body moving on pure instinct. Glass shatters around me, scattering like deadly confetti as I hurl myself toward cover.

Even as I seek refuge from the chaos unfolding around me, the harsh reality of the situation begins to sink in. The crashing and wailing sirens seem to converge, wrapping me in a suffocating blanket of noise and confusion. Panic gnaws at the edges of my mind, threatening to enclose me in a persistent wave of overwhelming fear.

Fighting against the rising tide of darkness working diligently to consume me, I push back against the overwhelming surge of panic taking over my senses. I force myself to focus, to keep moving forward despite the odds stacked against me.

Just when it seems like things couldn't possibly get any worse, the flickering beacon of light at the end of the tunnel vanishes without warning, eclipsing me into suffocating silence. The alarms fall quiet, leaving behind an eerie stillness that hangs heavily in the air. My lungs tighten, and nausea sets in.

It's so dark, I fear for just a second that I must have fallen into a familiar realm of unconsciousness. Though, when I instinctively grab the walls of the tunnel, my fingers are met with the unique texture once again, confirming that I am still awake. I am still here.

The power source has failed.

Chapter Six

The Fractured Sky

With the light at the end of the tunnel gone, I have to keep pressing forward the best I can without a guide to follow. Thankfully, there are no other turns, and my path is one straight shot to where I remember the exit to be.

I pound myself into the ground and know I have to be getting closer. My oxygen plate alarm is still beeping assertively as my breaths maintain their same unsteady rhythm. After what feels like an eternity, I run into the same vines I pulled away when I entered. Their tingly feeling against my face makes me step back temporarily as I unexpectedly run into them in the darkness.

Grabbing them and ripping them away from me more violently than necessary, I scramble my way out and feel around in the disturbing blackness until I find my drawstring propped neatly where I had left it. I pull apart the tight opening and reach inside for my glow torch. Searching around in circles, my hand finally wraps around the firm handle, and I instantly snatch it from beneath my sketchbook and flip the switch. I don't think I could ever be more thankful for not forgetting it this time.

Instantly, the life around me is more visible once again, though only within a few feet' radius of the soft glow. The rumbling never stops, and both far in the distance and way above me, I hear the sound of cracking and tearing. Large objects are falling, so much is breaking everywhere. The sky is actually falling. I never imagined that phrase could be used so literally. To say I am terrified is an understatement.

My eyes are wide as I stand and scan everywhere. Without the overhead light showing me my surroundings, I don't know which direction I came from. The reality has proven to be rather difficult to accept, but I know I have to face it.

I am lost.

My panicked gaze scans the large plants and unfamiliar ground. Still, I can't remember which path is my way out. I need to get out, and I know I need to run. Without power, there is no light. Not just any light, but rather, there is no sunlight. There is no more energy, and nothing can live here either. I don't have a choice—I just run. I run as fast as my body will let me. My lungs burn with the force I put them through, but I have to get out of Caddell.

I don't have time or space in my frantic mind to consider whether or not I'm going the way I need to anymore. My glow torch flickers at the pace of my heart rate through the wind as I drive myself through the brush. I need to keep going.

Before I see it, I can hear it coming. The sound cuts through the dark like a dagger, each step pounding like a countdown to my doom. I skid to a stop and freeze. My oxygen monitor screams at me, each beep a frantic warning as I hold my breath, so horrified at what is about to come. My heart thunders in my chest, my mind a tornado of fear and desperation.

I hold the torch above my head and turn my head up. Just as I do, I am met with a few feet' distance that holds for less than a second of my view. Panic surges through me, electrifying my limbs with a strange feeling of partial numbness. I lunge forward to get away, but it's too late.

The light comes down to the side, luckily, but the explosion of glass is bound to make contact with me. I trip on a large stick of some kind that catches me from being able to make a full motion away from the crash. I fall face-first and begin to roll. I tumble and scrape myself on the hard floor as I go. Once the spinning stops, I feel my back hit hard against the stump of a tree. Somehow, I have landed myself in a near-sitting position, managing not to hit my head with some form of pure luck.

I try to be strong; I really do. It all happens so fast I don't have a chance to feel any pain. But when I do come to and realize what has just happened, I know, even in the faint glow of my torch that now lies on its side a couple of feet from where I rest, my skin has turned pale.

"I don't want to, I don't want to... no, no, no, I can't do this! I can't!" I yell out loud as if someone else could hear me in the vast emptiness. Not only do I yell in hopes of being heard, but also so I can find a spark of hope within myself to try and calm down and take care of myself. I have to look. I know I have to.

“Agghhh!” I shriek as I tilt my head down to analyze my right shoulder. The tears are fogging the remaining sight I have left, but I can still see it. There’s a cut through my shoulder that nearly has my arm taken from my body. It’s still there, but barely. The cut is deep. I realize now why the pain isn’t there. I can’t feel it. I can barely feel anything.

The sharp glass edge shot through me so fast, I didn’t even realize it happened as I rolled down here. The blood begins seeping onto my lap, and I feel it soaking into my pants. Its disturbing warmth meets my cold skin beneath the suit.

“Help me! Please, someone, please be there! Please!” I know no one is there.

I am going to *die*.

This is my instant thought, of course, being the stress case I am. My biggest fear is death. I think many people are scared of it, but as someone who has seen it before, I know it is something I dread ever experiencing again. I don’t want to die yet. I can't be here alone, I can't be. I can't be here without...

My thoughts trail off. "Jess!" I scream for her. I don't just want her; I need her.

"Please, Jess, please I... I can't be alone! I was never made to be alone, Jess, please!" She is my everything. "I’m here, Jess! I’m here, please help me!" I let my voice fizzle out.

All I can do is hope that somehow she hears me, that at least someone hears me out through the blackness surrounding me. I grit my teeth and grasp my shoulder with my left hand. Instantly, I am greeted by the warm liquid as it seeps between my fingers.

You know the saying, "Be careful what you wish for?" I thought that was so fake, so unimportant in all of reality. I would do anything to get my wish, absolutely anything. Now I realize it's been true all along. I always wanted to be set free, and maybe it is time for me to get my wish. Only, it is nothing as I had intended it to be.

I feel my intense mentality slowly beginning to relax while I drift. My vision starts to blur as I feel myself slipping further from consciousness, and that's when I start to see her running toward me. Her gorgeous hair bounces as she runs in seemingly slow motion. She is so beautiful.

As she nears, I swear that I can feel her soft hands reaching out and touching over my mask, moving the hair away from my eyes like she always loves to do.

I close my eyes.

Chapter Seven

Welcome Home

"James! James! Oh God, please, come on, James, wake up! James, come on, it's me, Jess! Wake up, please! Oh, JJ, please!" Her voice penetrates through me, bouncing around in my head. It seems so real. It's crazy what the mind can make you think, or even see. She is so close, so close that I can almost feel her.

And then I realize I can.

My body leans forward from the tree as I open my eyes. I have to think about it again just to make sure it is really happening. I am able to see her tear-soaked brown eyes in front of my face, meeting mine once again. She straddles herself over me and runs her hands all over my face. I have never seen her look like this before. She is smiling now through the wetness surrounding her eyes, drops sticking to her lashes.

"Oh, JJ, you're okay! You're okay, I promise!" She laughs with a sound of relief as she cries with joy, and my lungs regain their strength. I am too focused on my new breath at first to be able to say anything to her. I am still in shock that I am here, and so is she.

I allow myself to fall into her, angling my head down as she grabs the sides of my face and leans her forehead into mine. We both close our eyes as we cry with a shared line of the miracle that keeps us together. I rub my forehead back and forth slightly against hers as she holds me, her soft hands brushing through my hair.

After moments of taking in every little bit of oxygen I can, I glance down at my shoulder. She has it all wrapped firmly so I can no longer see the blood or damage done. My oxygen plate looks to be in perfect condition as well. Jess is trained in medical aid; she works hard, and she's excellent at what she does. She actually is the one assigned to treat all of us in emergency situations.

All of us.

The higher level of realization begins to set through me. Where is everyone? What about the Ripple, and my dad? Where is my dad? I have so many questions, but that's when the more overwhelming thought crosses me. The lights are back on. I was so focused on everything but the power that I nearly forgot all about it being out.

"Jess..." I pull my head up from her grasp. She leans back slightly and moves herself from over me to the side, sitting close still. Through the mask blocking her beautiful smile from my sight, I can see it all through the spark she holds in her eyes.

"Yes, my sweet boy? God, I was so worried about you, James. I... you know what, never mind. You're okay now." I watch as a single tear forms and falls to the ground as she tries to keep her composure after nearly losing me.

“What...” My voice trickles, and I clear my throat and inhale deeply before resuming. “What happened? Where is everyone?”

"Oh, JJ..." Her voice trails off, a mixture of concern and disbelief evident in her tone as she observes my frantic action. With a swift movement, I raise my arm, the familiar weight of my watch comforting yet ominous, a constant reminder of the impending deadline I have been anxiously counting down to for what feels like an eternity.

9:54 A.M.

The digits glow a faint red against the dimly lit room, each blink seeming to taunt me with the passage of time. My heart races, and I shake my head in denial, unable to comprehend that it could all be over so soon. The air feels thick with tension, and the sound of my own ragged breaths fills the space around me, drowning out any other noise.

"There's no way it's all over already," I mutter to myself, the words barely audible over the rapid thumping of my heart. But as another minute slips by, the reality of the situation begins to sink in, sending a surge of panic coursing through my veins.

Before I could spiral further into despair, her hand clasps around my trembling wrist, grounding me in the present moment. "Hey, no, no, no, you're not going to freak out on me, okay?" Her voice is firm, yet laced with empathy.

“Look at me, James, please.” She knows I could never say no to her. I leave the fixation I had on the watch and find her soft eyes. I cough as I try to calm my oxygen pace to normal levels as she explains.

"Nobody knows exactly what happened, but it seems as though the area must have been a target for some sort of earthquake as a result of the increasing pressure from the beginning stages of the atmosphere opening. I don't know how no one saw it coming, but nothing predicted it." She reaches her hand back up against the side of my face and allows me to rest my head into her palm. This is practically a different Jess; she never lets me in like this. She is stubborn and never likes to be too close to anyone.

"The lights all went dark not long before I stepped into this place looking for you, which is beneficial anyway because the power outage caused the emergency locks on the doors to release, which allowed me to open the door without it being sealed. Instinctively, though, I shut the door back once I was in, sealing me inside. Let's just say I am really glad you were for sure in here too." She half-laughs, a feeling of gratitude knowing that she wasn't trapped in here alone.

That makes two of us now.

"The power stayed out until about twenty minutes ago, but it was too late. The Ripple already happened, and everything was falling apart out there. I had to sew your arm with just the light from your torch." She continues explaining while I attempt to keep listening. I can't believe what she is saying, what is actually happening. None of this was planned. Everything we ever do is followed by a plan.

Seeing my confusion, she tries to help me understand more. "You were in shock, JJ, and your shoulder is badly hurt. You're lucky you're still alive." She rubs my good arm slightly in a comforting manner as we continue. It all seemed so real to me, though. I must have had one heck of a panic attack if I hallucinated my own lungs giving out.

"Your dad stayed behind to see what's happening. He knows nothing will make it if he doesn't at least try. Your tracker showed that you were in your room, and I, of course, was the first one to go and find out that you were gone. I didn't get the chance to tell your father, or anyone else. I just knew I had to find you." I don't think I've ever heard pain in Jess's voice like this before. She is an emotional sway of pure thankfulness for my survival and grieving from the loss of everyone stuck beyond the door.

"I knew I would find you here. I don't know why—I just had this... feeling, I guess." We look at each other once again as she picks her lost gaze up from the ground and back to me. I want to say something, but I don't want to stop her from telling me more.

"They all were frantic, and I ran through the halls in the opposite direction. I parted from them and ran straight to Caddell." Her voice carries a deep concern I wish I could take from her.

"I'm so glad I did, JJ. I'm so sorry I wasn't here sooner." She ruffles my hair again before standing and brushing off. She is clean and prepared for the big day, and now it has resulted in her being covered in traces of my blood speckled onto her.

This is all my fault.

"I'm sorry, Jess, so sorry." It takes a ton not to crack my voice as I speak. She just shakes her head and reaches down to me, motioning for me to grab her arm with the one functioning one I have left.

"Never be sorry for making me care about you, JJ," she smirks with her eyes as she wipes away her tears and leans down to help me find my balance.

With team effort, I find my feet and stand up once again. Just a moment ago, I thought I would never be able to do that ever again. I thought I would possibly never see her again either, but all because of her, I'm still here.

We both are.

She wraps her arm around me as I stand in an awkward stance, my coordination slightly hindered, and I begin to feel the pain I should have felt long ago in my shoulder. I wince slightly but try to straighten myself. I want to be strong, not for myself, but for her. I need to be strong for her.

"You know what this means, right?" Her always uplifting tone lightens even the darkest of times. As we begin to walk, I can't help but turn and look at her once again.

"Yes, Jessica?" I speak to her. She smiles so big beneath her mask, and honestly, it has never felt better to joke with her. I love making her laugh, or rather, making her mad in most cases. I know deep down she always likes it, though.

"It's officially just me and you now. No rules, no others. Your father... he can't stop you anymore." She pauses as she speaks, and I am still putting together each piece of what she just said. She is right. It truly is just us now. For the first time, there aren't any rules to follow. There aren't any others to share our resources and tasks with. I can't bring myself to fully accept that he is gone.

"I guess I was too busy trying not to die to even think about it all still, but you're right." She beams back at me as I turn back to focus on the path in front of us.

We keep walking in sync through the vegetation and on toward the Center Port House. I don't know what to say, or think. My father is gone, and I should be sad, not content... right? But, after everything he has done to me, I can't help but find a little sliver of peace in being free from his dark shadow casting over me.

Peace.

It isn't the same as what I feel with the glowing edges through the tunnel. I don't know what that was, but it can't compare to this. I am here, in a world I never got to appreciate for its true beauty before. I thought I was okay to leave it all before, but I know now there are far bigger things I still need to do, so much more I still need to see. There's still so much more left for me to live for.

"We're free. We're finally free," I whisper, the words heavy with the weight of years of captivity. My voice trembles with a mixture of relief and disbelief as I keep my head bowed, unable to meet her gaze. Something still doesn't feel quite right, like this can't really be happening.

As we attempt to get ourselves moving forward away from this area, I remember my drawstring has to be nearby. Given the pain that's eating away at my core, I normally wouldn't care to leave behind anything. But this sketchbook is different. I've drawn everything in that book. Everything I was, everything I am, and everything I will be.

"Hey, wait, did you see my bag near here by chance?" I turn to take in my surroundings, but the dizziness causes my head to spin, resulting in blurred, useless vision.

Jess pauses, her eyes scanning the ground around us. "Your bag? Oh, right, hold on a second." She walks a few steps away, her movements swift and deliberate.

I lean against a nearby tree, trying to steady myself. The pain is relentless, but the thought of losing my sketchbook is even more unbearable. Each page holds a piece of my soul, an object containing all of the emotions I've never voiced.

Jess returns, holding my bag with a triumphant smile. "Found it! Here you go."

"Thanks," I mutter, my voice barely above a whisper. My breath is still unsteady, my body aches as I shift. I reach out and take the bag from her, my fingers trembling slightly. Opening it, I rummage through until I feel the familiar edges of my sketchbook. Relief floods through me as I pull it out.

Jess watches me, her expression softening. "You know, you never did show me any of your drawings," she says gently. "I can tell they mean a lot to you."

I glance at her, then back at the sketchbook. The thought of showing her my drawings goes through my mind each and every day, and it always feels both terrifying and liberating. I want to show her, I want someone to see what I've created all this time here.

"Yeah, they do. It's... it's how I express myself."

She nods, understanding in her gaze. "Whenever you're ready, I'd love to see them."

I manage to crack a small smile back into my eyes, tucking the sketchbook safely back into my bag. "Maybe one day."

"Take your time," she says reassuringly. "We have forever."

Her voice hung in the air as I snapped further away from my focus on the drawings and back into the current moment.

"But for now, let's get out of here. We need to keep moving and get you to the Center Port House." Her voice pushes me on, stopping me from dwelling too much on the true impact of the few words she previously stated.

Forever.

I nod, a better feeling, a surge of determination. As we begin to walk, I hold my drawstring close to me with my one good arm. Having my sketchbook secure and Jess by my side, the pain feels a little more bearable. We press on, each step taking us further away from this place, but closer to whatever comes next.

I still have so many questions, so much I need to know, though. If only my strong arm wasn't nearly parted from me and I could just sit and peacefully draw right now. I could draw the weights stacked on my shoulders, each representing a different responsibility this means we now are both stuck with. Me and Jess, lying beneath a pile of boulders crushing down while we stand alone in a world we were never born to be in.

As we make our way further from my resting point, the drawing becomes more and more detailed in my mind. Usually, my drawings have something to do with my father. But this time, the ideas are spiraling more around my head with the actuality of him not being here.

He can't stop me anymore. He can't *hurt* me anymore.

The thoughts echo heavily through my mind. I have broken free from the chains that bound me. With each step, I take off the cuffs of his control. The memories of his hands holding me down, his words cutting me like knives, still haunt me, but they no longer hold the power they once did. I am no longer just James, the shell of a person I became under his influence. I am something more, something stronger.

Almost as though a glimpse of purpose is shifting within me, a faint flicker of hope igniting in the darkness of my past. I dare to believe that I can find peace, not just for myself, but for Jess too. She stands by me through it all; her unwavering support is a beacon of light in my darkest hours without her even realizing it.

"You're right," I murmur, the weight of those words settling heavily on my shoulders.

She turns over her shoulder, eyes meeting mine once again. “About what?”

"If he’s really gone, and I am the only Caddell left, doesn’t that mean I must bear the burden of this place now?" The realization hits me like a freight train, knocking the breath from my lungs.

We both pause, stopping and taking in the moment. The air is thick with unspoken tension as we lock eyes. I can feel her gaze probing, searching for any flicker of emotion that might betray the storm raging within me. It's as if she's peering into the depths of my soul, unraveling the tangled web of thoughts and feelings that churn beneath the surface. I wish my emotions wouldn’t vary as much as they do, and that I didn’t need to draw to tell even myself what it is that I feel, but I can't help it. Speaking my emotions never was part of who I am.

For a moment, the world falls away, leaving only the two of us standing in the quiet intensity of the moment. I can almost hear the thumping of my own heartbeat, a steady rhythm that pulses in time with the unspoken emotions that hang heavily in the air between us. In her eyes, I see a reflection of myself. The fragmented glimpse is enough to make me look away for a moment and gather the strength to speak again.

"This is my home... No, not just my home, Jess. This is our home." I speak more clearly than I had previously, as my airway is clear and I take it all in as I form my words. She stands there with me in silence, her brown eyes fading from curiosity, still tense from the accident I faced just moments before now turning into a feeling of comfort. She doesn't deserve to carry any of the boulders; I want to let her rest all of her burdens on me. We can finally do everything together.

Her brows lift slightly, and her lower eyelid drops slowly. She steps one more foot forward, closer to me, and her sight aligns at the same height as mine.

"Well then, James Caddell, I guess it's only appropriate for me to be the first to tell you this once again." Taken in by her use of my real full name, now that there is no one stopping her from calling me that, I can't help but admire her even more. My heart falls further back into my chest, a feeling I haven't quite figured out how to explain. I know what she is going to say before she even opens her mouth, hiding beneath the material blocking me from seeing her contagious grin.

"Welcome home."

Chapter Eight

Pinky Promise

Emerging from the dense tangle of bushes, we finally arrive at the familiar pathway leading to the Center Port House. This place, with its imposing presence, always gives me a sense of discomfort. The way it seems to pulsate, as if it were alive, makes my stomach churn. Despite my aversion to the house, the persistent ache in my shoulder urges me to seek refuge within its walls. Just the thought of lying down on a bed seems like an oasis in the desert of my exhaustion.

As we walk, the ground around the house is covered with a carpet of purple plants. These plants are unlike any I have seen before above. They resemble grass but are shorter, with delicate, rounded petals instead of sharp blades. With each step, the petals gently flatten under our feet, creating a soothing sensation as we move forward.

As Jess and I stroll through the soft flowers, she begins bringing up a moment from her childhood, something she rarely ever talks about. "You know," she starts, her voice carrying a nostalgic tone,

"I just realized I never told you the full story about the time my family went camping when I was twelve, did I?"

I glance at her, curious. "Not the details, no. Just about how much you love the color purple because of it. I guess I never asked you why, though."

She shrugs, a wistful smile playing on her lips. "I guess it just never came up. Anyway, we were in this beautiful valley surrounded by mountains. The air was crisp, and the sky was painted with a million stars."

I nod, picturing the scene in my mind. "Sounds magical."

"It was," she agrees, her eyes sparkling with the memory. "But the best part was the morning after we arrived. I woke up before everyone else and decided to take a walk around the campsite. That's when I stumbled upon this gorgeous field of purple flowers."

I raise an eyebrow, intrigued. "Like, real purple flowers? I've only ever seen true flowers in a floral shop on the street in New York. Did they look anything like these weird little purple dots we're stepping on?"

Jess shakes her head eagerly. "Exactly! That's what made them so special. They were these tiny, delicate flowers that covered the ground like a blanket. And when you walked on them, they'd flatten under your feet, like a natural carpet. They were nearly identical to these."

I smile at the image she paints. "Interesting. They really are pretty." I wish I had the self-confidence to tell her they still weren't as pretty as she is.

"Purple quickly became my favorite color after that day," her voice is soft with nostalgia. "I remember feeling so connected to the world in that moment, like I was part of something bigger than myself." She keeps looking at the flowers as we continue. Lost in our conversation and the memories, it's moments like these that remind me how lucky I am to have Jess as my best friend.

We cross diagonally across the field of tiny purple flowers toward the entrance. The walls are a series of reflecting green lights, just like our suits, picking up every drop of false sunlight from above. The outer edges groan as they slightly sway, working hard to create the valuable energy we need to survive.

"Ah, she's a beauty, isn't she? Kinda cute, right?" I can't contain my sarcasm. Jess, with her ever-playful demeanor, responds in her characteristic fashion, her tone laced with subtle amusement. "That's one word for it, I guess."

Her words linger in the air, teasingly playful, yet carrying a depth of meaning that only Jess can convey. It's one of those moments where her response speaks volumes, saying everything and nothing at the same time.

Standing at the glass door, we can barely see through the tint blocking a clear view. Standing on those steps is something we've both done so many times, but everything feels unfamiliar and new again.

We embark on the delicate task of entering the facility. As I approach the imposing glass door, its surface reflects bright beams into my eyes under the artificial lighting, causing me to hesitate for just a moment. With an unsteady hand, I grasp the cold metal zipper that runs along the edge.

I unfasten the zipper, and the metallic sound echoes in the quiet corridor with Jess by my side, offering silent support. Together, we step through the threshold, the transition from outside to inside marked by a crisp shift in atmosphere. As I begin to close the door behind us, a sudden, searing pain erupts across my chest, catching me off guard.

For a quick moment, I am frozen in place, and my body is locked in a reflexive response to the intensity of the sensation. I fight to maintain composure, suppressing the urge to cry out as the pain radiates through every fiber inside me. It feels as though invisible claws are running through my chest, leaving me breathless and vulnerable in the dimly lit entrance. With a discomforting effort, I manage to regain control.

Her comforting voice is a familiar melody of reassurance that wraps around me tightly as she leans in closer. With gentle care, she extends a supportive hand, guiding me as I struggle to regain my upright posture. Each movement is a battle against the persistent ache that pulses and the never-ending darkness that radiates between my flesh and bones.

"Yeah," I muster, my voice strained, "it just... hurts." The words escape me in short gasps, each syllable a clear sign of the sharp sting that shoots through me with every breath. Each inhalation feels like needles pricking through my skin.

"Here, let me finish this one. Start heading to the cleaning chamber." She gently moves me to the side and goes behind me to finish sealing the first door.

I start toward the cleaning chamber, using slow and gentle steps. It is starting to get a little easier to breathe without as severe pain again as I stand straight. I am almost to the entrance when Jess catches up and comes running next to me.

Entering the second glass doorway, there lies another metal zipper, and yet again, a series of Jess helping me through, both opening and shutting the seal this time. The room is bright, and the lights instantly start to hurt my head.

The decontamination chamber stands as a filtration system against the intrusion of foreign particles, thoughtfully engineered to protect our precious food supplies from any potential contamination brought in from the outside world. As we step inside, a sense of anticipation tingles in the air, mingling with the faint scent of sterile cleanliness. With a quiet hum, the chamber springs to life, consuming us in a swirling mist of pure white.

The dense fog obscures our vision, enveloping us in a blanket of vapor, while the room echoes with the soft hiss of cleansing agents at work. Despite the close proximity, our figures dissolve into mere silhouettes, faint outlines in the billowing clouds.

Minutes pass in a haze, the atmosphere thick with anticipation and the lingering sensation of purification. Then, as swiftly as it descends, the mist dissipates, revealing the pristine interior of the chamber once more. Surprisingly, there is no stinging in our eyes, no discomfort from the cleansing agents that have just enveloped us. It always bothers my eyes when I come in here; I wonder why it doesn't hurt now. Maybe it has something to do with my injuries. Instead, there is only a lingering feeling of dryness, a contrast to the apparent moisture that had surrounded us moments before.

Jess is rubbing her eyes as we near the exit into the main lobby, and I feel her just barely run into my back as we make our way out, though she pretends nothing happened. I elect not to make fun of her this time.

As we stroll through the lobby, the soft glow of overhead lights casting warm pools of illumination on the polished floor, she glances over at me with a playful tilt of her head.

"You hungry?" Her voice is laced with a hint of teasing, the question hanging in the air like a tantalizing invitation as we make our way toward the kitchen.

I let out a groan, a dramatic flourish to accompany my response. "No way. My stomach feels like it could fall on the floor, and somehow, I would feel better." With a wince, I clutch my abdomen, as if trying to physically convey the discomfort gnawing within. But she isn't about to let me off the hook that easily. A knowing smirk tugs at the corners of her lips as she arches an eyebrow in disbelief.

"Yeah, right. You didn't complain once this whole time about your stomach hurting." Her words carry a playful challenge, a tone that only comes from years of friendship. She sees right through my feeble attempt to avoid the truth, a reminder that some things can never be hidden from those who know us best.

"Okay, well, can you just accept that I'm not hungry? Definitely not for that grub right now. Can I just get some sleep instead for today, doctor?" I'm not entirely lying. I mean, my stomach is uneasy from the pain. Simply the thought of eating from this place right now is nauseating.

The task seems simple: on our left abdomen region is a clasped closed tube. We have to place that tube into a bowl of mushy, yellowish-green paste that it sucks up like a vacuum cleaner. It's honestly so disgusting I sometimes question starving to death.

"Fine, but you have to eat tomorrow. You lost a ton today. Let's get you to bed then, stubborn." I watch her use both of her hands to flip her hair over her shoulders, allowing a wave of shiny brown to flow effortlessly down her back.

As we pass by the kitchen table, we both take a moment to set down our carrying items and sit them down neatly together. I'm quicker and less caring about my materials, so it only takes me a matter of seconds to throw my bag on the table.

I stand there for what seems like an eternity, admiring her while she takes a few minutes just to make sure her tubes are straight and her mask is completely together as she carefully takes off her medical supplies. Her expression is one of the most interesting things I have ever seen as she remains focused. I wish I could see the rest of her face.

As I fumble with my bag, pretending to organize its contents, my mind churns with confusion and longing. A common thought crosses my mind: Do I love her? The concept of love is as foreign to me as the surface world I've grown to forget. The movies I watched as a child, before everything went south, always showed couples in close embraces, whispering sweet words and pressing their faces together in a way that seemed somehow natural. I always thought it was just fantasy, a distraction from the harsh reality. Yet, here I am, feeling something so intense it scares me. My chest tightens when she's near, forcing me to hold my breath without consent. It's truly terrifying what just her presence can do to me.

I try to dissect these feelings, wondering if it's just a desperate need for connection in this desolate existence, or if it's something deeper, something that I guess could be called love. But how can I know for sure? Every instinct engraved into me is about survival, not emotional vulnerability. She glances up at me, but before she can catch me staring, I move my sight elsewhere.

"Oh, right, I should probably take those off, huh?" I pretend to look down at my feet as if I have been thinking about untying my boots in the moments I have been looking at her. I reach down, pulling them free with a single tug and placing them to the side of the table.

"Probably best to sleep without boots on," she says back and heads down the hall. I follow closely behind her to my room.

Once inside the lovely room number 015, matching the same number assigned to me for ages as one of The Selected, I limp my way quickly over to the bed. Sitting on the mattress causes me to produce an instant sigh of relief as the throbbing arm pain is slightly more relaxed.

"Never felt better," I say out loud, but I always have a habit of speaking too soon. Just as I go to breathe in fully, the cramping across my chest comes back. I elect to, therefore, turn on my left side and curl into a fetal position in the middle of the bed.

"Oh, JJ..." She comes over to the bed and runs her hand lightly down my arm. It hurts, don't get me wrong, but maybe I did decide to make it a bit more dramatic to get her to come closer.

"Do you..." I whimper in a more convincing manner. "Do you think you could stay here with me just for tonight?"

"JJ, I..." Her voice trails off as I grasp my chest harder as the pain resurfaces with my inhale after that last sentence. It hurts, don't get me wrong, but maybe I am being a tad bit dramatic to gain her empathy.

"Okay, but just for tonight. This isn't going to become a regular thing," she says. She doesn't wait for me to say anything else. Instead, she makes her way down to the end of the bed, pulling the covers off the ground and coming to lay next to me, laying the blanket over both of us. I can't help but feel the butterflies flying through me as she lays just one more inch closer. Suddenly, the hurt I hold is nowhere to be found.

"Goodnight, idiot. Try and get some rest," she says. I know she's smiling even with my back turned to her. I want more than anything to say how there's no possible way for me to sleep with her staying this close to me for so long, but I choose to keep my words simple.

"Goodnight, Jessica." Short and sweet, with a hint of sarcasm. I don't want to press the limit too far. As I fade into my dream, I'm filled first with one of my favorite memories, one I've resorted back to so many times to step out of the darkness. Sometimes it's hard to remember that there's always a light somewhere; it just might need to be turned on.

I remember it all so vividly. Jess and I had been close friends for about a year at that point, and we were just starting to be more comfortable with talking more about our feelings rather than always just messing around. I had told her some about my goals, something I had even forgotten about myself until then.

I told her about how my dreams were to be an astronaut as a little kid. I loved the idea of spinning in space, all of the stars and planets floating without anything tying them down there. She told me how she wanted to become the best doctor in the world. We laughed some, but truly connected over our future ideas. We were stuck underground, in a place where our dreams would likely never be able to come true, yet we were still so hopeful.

I can still hear our conversation, her younger voice echoing through my slumbering mind. "Pinky promise me, JJ, that no matter what, we won't forget who we said we wanted to be one day?" She had a spark in her eye, something I lost long ago, but I was certain I could find again in that moment.

"Pinky promise." I grinned back at her, our pinky fingers locking in a vow that should never be broken.

This moment has stuck with me this far, and though it's seemingly impossible, I hope we never have to break our promise. I came here today to spend time alone, to figure out myself. I thought that by exploring without anyone else around, I would be able to see something. I was looking for who I was. I needed an answer; I needed to know who I am. I was looking for the boy I used to know, the one I will be, and the one I am right now, all at the same time. I've been battling no one but myself for as long as I remember.

If there is one thing that impacted me most from my unforgiving search, it's that I guess it really doesn't matter where you look.

It's how.

Chapter Nine

Maybe One Day

My dream only seems to last as long as the memory, and I soon find myself already awake again. It feels like I just blinked, and now it's over. I'm met again by the stabbing pain in my right shoulder. The pain is hard to describe; it feels like someone is taking a knife and pressing it into me before dragging the sharp tip over my chest. It's impossible to get comfortable again. I sit up and stretch, rubbing my chest with my functioning arm. As I expect, that's when I realize Jess is no longer sleeping next to me.

I rub my eyes and groan slightly as I bend sideways, trying to work out the pain. It's no use. I scoot my way to the end of the bed and find my feet placement. I walk over to the glass exit door, and as I could've put money on, there she is, sitting on the ledge with her legs dangling over the edge. Her feet are just a few centimeters from touching the purple plants below.

She looks deep in thought. Jess doesn't have relatives here who were taken yesterday like most of the people down here. She had her parents taken from her a long time ago. I think it's been about ten years now, if I'm not mistaken. They were both killed in a car crash, and Jess was in the car. Since then, she has devoted her life to understanding human medical aid to help others. She wants to do this for them, like somehow maybe she can fix others she loves because she wasn't able to save her own.

We all have our own secrets, just some of us show them differently.

I used to think about Mom a lot, and I'd be lying if I said I didn't think about her as The Ripple got closer, and now that it's already happened. But I chose to stop letting her haunt me long ago when I accepted that she is the one who left me. She didn't just leave me, though. She made me stuck with that thing of a dad I've been forced to not only live with but also somehow respect above everyone else.

"Enough history lessons, James," I mumble to my inner self, trying to snap myself back to reality. I decide I need to stop being helpless and do something for her instead. As much as I don't want to, I decide to mosey my way into the kitchen. Once at the counter, I reach over, slide a bowl under the dispenser, and watch the thick green substance make its way out of the tube.

"Ehhh..." I can't help myself. It's so thick and chunky and ew.

I need to gain my own motivation somehow. I slip the tube switch off and count down from three before plugging in and unclasping my fancy Vivi armis tube, placing it into the bowl, sending the so-called meal into my system as quickly as possible. It's absolutely disgusting, and every time the suit gains nutrients, it feels as though my skin is literally crawling. At least now, when she asks, I get to tell her that I chose to do something against my will just for her. I adjust my mask and tubes, ensure they're plugged in accordingly, and briskly make my way to the door, zipping the seal promptly as I head out.

"Good morning, sugar! Never would I expect Jess Mercer to be up this early," I say in the most sarcastic tone possible. She is the earliest riser I've ever known.

I watch as she shakes her head, blinking a few times before looking up at me. "Says you! It's not even that early, dingus. You slept in, and I decided not to wake you."

"You see, it would be better if someone would stay with me all night like they said they would, but this is why we don't make promises around here, right?" I say it more jokingly than I really want to. I just can't understand why she won't let me in.

"I'm sorry, JJ, I just—" I cut her off before she finishes explaining to me. She lost the people she loved most when she was really young, and I know for a fact that must affect her ability to give all of her trust to anyone else.

"No need to explain to me, Jess, I'm messing with you!" I run, or rather walk at a faster pace than normal with my sore shoulder. I hop over the ledge and roll myself into the purple plants below.

"What are you doing?" She laughs and grabs the edges of the ledge she sits firmly on.

"What does it look like I'm doing? I've always wanted to roll around in these things! They're soft. You should give it a try!" I continue to gently toss myself around, careful not to land too hard on my wound.

"You're covered in purple, silly!" I love it when she sounds like that, all high-pitched. I know it means I have captured her full attention.

I roll over and lay on my back, my head facing in line with where she is sitting, which causes me to have to look at her from an upside-down point of view. She giggles as I bend back and look at her. I can see the purple dust stuck to my lashes, and it makes me chuckle a bit myself. I must look so dumb.

“I like seeing you like this, JJ,” she smiles at me through her shimmering amber eyes.

"Like what? Sticky and gross, all tangled in cords with stains on my clothes? Didn’t realize that’s all I had to do this entire time." I roll over onto my belly so I can see her without being upside down and give her my most iconic smirk. I add in a more devious expression this time as I lift my right eyebrow slightly higher than my left.

"No, you idiot. I like seeing you happy. I know you say you're happy ‘anytime you're with me,’ but this is different. This is exactly what I saw had been taken from you the day I met you. It’s like your spark was gone, but truly, for the first time, I think it’s finally making its way back." She always knows how to make words sound so good. It makes me jealous.

"Maybe one day I could say something that sounds at least half as poetic as what you just threw out, but thank you anyway for saying that." I tilt my head loosely to the left, my soft wavy hair flopping to the side with me as I turn.

"Or, maybe one day you'll stop saying stuff like that and start taking life a bit more seriously," she says in a way that I know she isn't being too stern, yet she still manages to get me thinking about all of my life choices.

Maybe one day, is that all I do? I feel like everything I say, every little reason I have for everything, is always placed into the category of 'I can never do that' in my head, and then I don't even try. I really need to get some of that stuff referred to as self-confidence.

"I'm working on it," is the best response I can come up with. I don't want her to think I'm a depressed bum all the time.

"Good." She tosses back while getting off the ledge she is sitting on, her posture switching to her classic, more formal standing position. "Now, you wanna go do something? I mean, besides rolling on the ground?"

I work myself back up into a criss-cross sitting position. "Well, what exactly do you have in mind, wise lady?"

"Do you ever stop? I mean seriously, do you?" She laughs and comes over to help my lazy self up off the ground. They taught us so many life skills, but no one thought to teach us how to push ourselves off the ground with one arm.

She reaches down to help pull me, but instead, I use my remaining strength to bring her to the ground without her expecting it. She falls onto my chest and rolls onto her back. I can't help but laugh as she tries to maintain her persistent attitude, but her actions show otherwise.

“You’re such an idiot, James, gosh! Seriously?” She sits up and immediately starts wiping as much of the lavender powder off of her skin-tight suit as best as she can.

“I couldn’t help myself! You’re the one who asked if I ever stop, so I just needed to clarify that we both understand the answer to that.” She wants to be mad, but she can’t help but giggle a frustrated laugh before shoving my forehead back and standing up, reaching her hand down for me to grab onto once again. This time, I reluctantly grab on and get up with her.

"Well, before you so rudely interrupted my thoughts, I was going to explain to you where I think we should go, but I guess you'll just have to wait and see." She catches herself, moving from my eyes and down to our hands, still interlocked as one from her helping me up just seconds before, as she talks. I see it too, and I know she doesn't like the idea of me seeing her thinking that way.

She quickly removes her soft fingers from mine and once again uses her hands to shake the remaining dust from her pants. I don't know why she always has to hide. Even now, when we are finally alone, she can't accept what she feels. I know she has to feel the same way—at least, I think she does.

"Go on, lead the way. The tour guide shoes are all yours." I beam at her over the top of my mask. She gives me a little nudge before we proceed away from the house and into the distinct world around us.

"Oh, and before you ask, I already ate this morning. Just for you, so don't think I did it for my own good," I clarify with her, though I am a little disappointed she hasn't asked me if I had already.

"I'm impressed. Let's go then, shall we?" She turns around and continues away from the house.

I follow closely behind her, ensuring my steps match nearly identically to hers. She knows her way around this place better than anyone.

Chapter Ten

The Anchor

Not long after we bid farewell to the protective confines of the Center Port House, our journey leads us into a dense forest of towering trees adorned with thick, textured bark the color of deep, regal purple. Each tree seems to rise effortlessly from the earth, their trunks standing proudly before abruptly angling sideways at a perfect right angle, defying gravity in a display of natural wonder.

The trunks boast impressive girth, their wide bases providing stability as they stretch upward toward the canopy above. Their sheer size and unique growth pattern transform our passage through the forest into more of a climbing expedition than a leisurely stroll. Each step requires careful navigation as we clamor over gnarled roots.

"'Hey... uh, Jess, where exactly are we going?" I intend to sound less formal in my tone, but instead, I just give a worried impression.

"Why, you scared to step over a couple of logs?" Her voice carries a teasing lilt, like a playful melody amidst the rustling leaves. I can't help but grin at her playful jab, knowing she'll find enjoyment in my momentary concern.

"Ha ha, try climbing logs with a useless right arm," I retort, my words edged with a hint of snarl. There's a flicker of amusement in her eyes as she takes in my response, and I can't help but feel a surge of affection despite myself.

“Oh, that's a bummer! I almost forgot that arms are used for stepping over things.” Her laughter dances behind her words in the air like a melody.

I glance ahead, my gaze scanning the winding path that stretches out before us, disappearing into the dense foliage of the forest. "How much longer?" I can't help but whine.

"Do you always complain this much? You know what—never mind, don’t answer that.” She knows I have a snarky answer brewing before I can clear my throat and even try to speak.

"Remember that one time when we snuck into your room to play music at, like, 2:00 a.m.?" I bring it up, a mischievous grin spreading across my face. "You were so sure that Dad would catch us."

Jess rolls her eyes but can't hide her smile. "And you swore we wouldn't get caught. We almost didn't, too, until you decided to blast the speaker at full volume when your favorite song came on."

"Hey, you loved that song! You literally were dancing on the bed like a maniac," I chuckle, nudging her playfully with my good arm.

"Yeah, well, I was a kid. Now I have more refined tastes.”

"Sure you do," I tease back.

"But I distinctly remember you singing while using my hairbrush as a mic." I knew this was coming.

"Okay, now listen, I thought we both agreed never to mention that ever again." I can't help but shake my head at the embarrassing remembrance of my younger self.

She laughs, the sound ringing through the trees like a wind chime. "Alright, alright, maybe the middle-of-the-night dance party was one of the best times of my life, I'll admit. But don't spread that around; no one needs to know we both looked like complete fools."

"Your secret's safe with me," I assure her, glancing at her from the corner of my eye as we both take in the sarcasm, since there literally is no one else we could tell this to. The way her face lights up with laughter makes the ache in my arm cease to exist once again.

"So, what's the plan once we get to... wherever we're going?" I stay persistent, hinting at her to give me any clue as to what we're headed toward.

"Well, if I told you, it wouldn't be a surprise, would it?" she replies, her eyes twinkling with mischief. There's something about the way she holds herself, a blend of playful confidence and genuine intrigue, that keeps me guessing.

I sigh dramatically, earning another laugh from her. "Fine, lead on, fearless guide. Just don't get us lost."

"Trust me," she says, her tone shifting slightly, a soft seriousness creeping into her voice. "I know exactly where we're going."

We trudge through the dense forest, the undergrowth crunching beneath our boots with each step. The canopy filters the light above, casting shadows that dance across our path. Time seems to stretch endlessly as we navigate the labyrinth of trees, each one blending into the next in a seemingly endless procession. The air is filled with the earthy scent of moss and the occasional sound of dripping water.

As we walk, I steal glances at her, wondering what thoughts still are lying behind her calm demeanor. "Are you always this mysterious?" I ask, breaking the silence.

She chuckles, a sound that feels warm and familiar. "Only when I want to be. Keeps things interesting, don't you think?"

"Interesting is one word for it," I reply, shaking my head with a grin. "Though a map might be more reassuring."

She pauses for a moment, looking back at me with a smile that's equal parts reassuring and teasing. "Where's the fun in that? Besides, sometimes the best places can't be found on any map. You're the most imaginative person I know, you should know better than that."

Our steps instantly are forced into a halt as me both manage to see what we are nearing at exactly the same moment in time. We both turn and look at each other with wide eyes before getting a bit closer to see more.

In the center of the clearing, a colossal branch sprawls across the earth, its sheer size dwarfing everything around it. It bridges a sizable gap in the ground, forming a makeshift bridge over a deep crack that splits the earth beneath us. The contrast between the delicate surroundings and the imposing presence of the fallen tree limb creates a surreal tableau, freezing us in our tracks as we take in the scene before us.

"Wait here," she commands, her arm outstretched in front of me, her expression commanding obedience with a single, authoritative glare that speaks volumes of her confidence and control.

"Ok fine mom, I'm not a child. I'm perfectly capable of accompanying you." I retort, unable to suppress the irritation that bubbles within me whenever I feel patronized. I was trying to joke slightly, but saying that word takes me back somewhere I don't want to be.

"Okay, James, but for heaven's sake, if you so much as inch towards that branch and entertain any foolish ideas, I swear-" Her warning is cut short by my interruption.

"I won't, gosh, just relax," I interject, my tone dripping with impatience as I try to push back the waves of frustration rising within me. It irks me to no end when she assumes such a protective stance, as if I'm incapable of handling myself in any remotely hard situation.

"Fine," she replies curtly, her words laced with restrained annoyance, a clear indication that my response hasn't eased her concerns in the slightest. In hindsight, perhaps I should have kept my retorts to myself, but the pressure of the situation weighs heavily on my shoulders. Deep down, she knows that no matter her instructions, I inevitably do as I please.

"You think the vibrations earlier triggered...this?" My voice carries a note of genuine astonishment. "It seems likely," she replies, her tone laced with a mixture of certainty and wonder. As we near the beginning of the branching pathway, we slow our pace, drawn toward the edge where the trench yawns wide below us. Together, we lean forward, peering down into the abyss that stretches down forever. The depths seem to swallow the light, casting shadows that dance and flicker along the walls of the chasm.

Far below, the surface of the rushing water shimmers with an ethereal glow, scattered beams of light playing across its surface like a celestial ballet. The sight is both mesmerizing and intimidating. A reflexive gulp escapes my throat, the sound echoing faintly in the cavernous space around us.

I turn my gaze towards Jess, anticipating a reflection of the unease stirring within me as I edge closer to the imposing precipice. However, to my surprise, her countenance bears not the slightest hint of panic, but rather a profound sense of sorrow and disappointment. With a gentle touch, I grasp her shoulders, guiding her away from the edge, positioning myself squarely in front of her. She refuses to maintain eye contact and her gaze keeps drifting back to the ground.

"Hey, Jess, talk to me. I'm here for you," I urge her, my voice coated with concern. Yet, she remains fixated on the ground, unwilling to meet my gaze. "Please, look at me," I implore, hoping to establish a connection.

As she finally lifts her eyes to meet mine, a solitary tear wells in the corner of her left eye, threatening to spill over. Acting on instinct, I extend my hand, intending to brush away the tear with my thumb, only to have it swiftly rebuffed by her. In an instant, her sorrow morphs into palpable frustration.

"It's just not fair," she murmurs, her words tinged with a sense of profound injustice. I search her eyes, attempting to decipher the source of her pain. She's stubborn, yes, but I've never seen her act like this over anything. This isn't Jess.

"What's so important over there, anyway?" I try my best to comfort her, but whatever tactics I employ seem utterly futile.

"You wouldn't get it, JJ... I just need to show you. I've been harboring this secret for far too long." Her distress is palpable, and all I want is to alleviate it in any way possible.

"Would you consider explaining it to me, perhaps?" I attempt to convey an open-minded stance, though inwardly, I'm burning with curiosity, desperate to unravel the mystery. Jess's fervor for whatever it is has me intrigued like never before.

"No, JJ it's not something I can just explain. You have to see it," she insists, her hands trembling as she brushes away tears cascading down her cheeks. Witnessing her anguish tears at my heartstrings, compelling me to act, to do something, anything, to help her. She blinks rapidly, as if trying to prevent her tears from spilling.

Self-reproach gnaws at me viciously, as though I am nothing but a pitiful excuse of a person, a spineless creature unworthy of offering even a single hand of meaningful support. Yet, as Jess's distress unfolds before me, a surge of determination courses through my veins, banishing those shadows of cowardice that have long plagued my spirit.

"Let's go then," I declare, the words tumbling from my lips with a newfound boldness, laced with a flicker of fervor that even surprises me. It's as if a dormant ember within me has suddenly ignited into flame. If I'm being honest, I have no idea what just got into me.

"What?" Jess's gaze locks onto mine, her eyes wide with a mixture of confusion and tentative hope. It's as if she's searching for something in the depths of my soul, hoping to find some sort of answer in my gaze.

"You heard me. What are we waiting for?" My own voice sounds strangely confident, cutting through the haze of uncertainty that has clouded my thoughts for so long. In this moment, doubt ceases to exist, replaced by a singular focus on action. What is wrong with me? This is a whole new breed of James evolving through.

Without hesitation, I reach out, my hand extending toward her trembling form. As my fingers make contact, I can feel the tremors coursing through her body, a physical manifestation of the fear and uncertainty that grip us both. Gently, I pull her into the shelter of my arm, drawing her close with a sense of urgency that belies the danger of our situation. I prepare us to move as one.

"JJ, we can't!" she protests, but I silence her with a firm shake of my head. No longer will I allow fear to dictate my actions.

"I'm tired of fear controlling me," I declare, my voice resolute as I propel us forward, determined to defy the grip of apprehension and stand firm in the face of uncertainty.

"No, Jess, I want to go. Whatever it is that's out there, it means a lot to you, which makes it matter to me, too. I'm done with being told I can't." I can't believe what I just said; it almost sounds genuinely inspirational.

She turns to me, and as confident as she always is, I can see that she is still afraid to attempt to walk the branch. Heck, I truly am terrified, but none of that matters to me as much as how it feels to be on the other side with her. She is always quiet when she is unsure, which is rare.

As Jess's gaze lingers on me, a silent plea for reassurance, I feel the weight of responsibility settle heavily upon my shoulders. "I'll go first, you hold onto me, okay?" I offer, mustering a tone that sounds far more heroic than I ever truly feel. It's a facade I wear, a facade I desperately cling to in order to bolster my own faltering resolve.

"We will be okay," I add, the words ringing hollow even in my own ears. But I have to believe them, if only for Jess's sake. I have to be the anchor she needs in this moment of uncertainty.

With a final steeling of my nerves, I make my decision. Stepping onto the weathered branch, I focus my gaze intently on the ledge beckoning from the other end, a distant beacon of safety amidst the yawning abyss below. Every fiber of my being screams with apprehension, my heart thundering in my chest as doubts gnaw at the edges of my resolve.

The branch beneath my feet is worn smooth by the passage of time and the elements. I hesitate, a surge of doubt threatening to overwhelm me as I teeter on the choice of retreating. But then, I feel Jess's arms encircle me from behind, her grip firm and unwavering.

At this moment, her touch is all the reassurance I need. With a deep breath, I banish the lingering specter of fear and uncertainty, drawing upon some courage I never knew I possessed. This isn't just about me anymore; it's about being the strength Jess needs.

With newfound determination coursing through my veins, I edge near the base of the branch, my foot finding purchase on the trembling branch beneath me. I feel as though I'm stepping outside of myself as we take a step forward together.

No longer as two, but as one.

Chapter Eleven

Piggyback

As we slowly advance along the slender, swaying branch, every movement teeters between our short breaths. Each step carries the weight of uncertainty, a daring dance with fate above the roiling waters below. The surface of the river seethes beneath us, its dark embrace beckoning with a sinister allure. With every quiver of the branch beneath our feet, the tension in Jess's grasp around me amplifies, her fingers clenching with a silent urgency that mirrors the rhythm of my own apprehension.

I can feel Jess's trust in me growing with each passing moment. It's a fragile thing, easily shattered by the slightest misstep or miscalculation. But for now, we cling to it desperately, drawing strength from each other as we navigate.

"Steady now," I whisper, my voice strained with the effort of reassurance, battling against the tumultuous throb of my racing heart. "Just keep your grip tight. We're almost there." Each syllable hangs heavy in the air.

The thick, gnarled branch groans and strains beneath the added burden of our weight, its protest echoing through the stillness of the forest. Each creak seems to pierce the air like a warning, a constant reminder of the depths of our situation. With every sway, it feels as though we are teetering on the edge of life or death.

Suddenly, a snap echoes through the air, startling us both. Jess lets out a gasp, her grip tightening reflexively around my arm. My heart leaps into my throat, and for a moment, I freeze, fear gripping me like a vice. But then, with a wave of relief, I realize it's just a stray twig giving way somewhere above us.

"Are you okay?" I ask, my voice hushed with concern as I glance back at Jess.

Her eyes are wide with adrenaline. "Yeah, yeah, I'm fine. Just... just keep going."

With a silent nod, we press on, our determination forged stronger by the brief moment of terror. My entire being is consumed by the urgent task of maintaining my balance, a task made all the more challenging by the relentless sway of the branch.

I dare not glance down, for fear that the dizzying drop below will overwhelm me, dragging me into its depths. The waves below beckon with a silent, chilling call, threatening to swallow me whole if I allow myself to make even the slightest misstep.

Beside me, Jess's presence offers a fragile solace in the midst of our journey. Yet, it also serves as a constant reminder of the weight of responsibility resting upon my shoulders. Her silent apprehension hangs heavy in the air, a tension that strains the already tight silence between us. Each breath she takes seems to carry the weight of unspoken fears, adding to the burden that threatens to drag us down into the abyss.

"We're halfway there," I say, more to reassure myself than anything else. "Just a little farther."

With each step, the distance to solid ground seems to stretch on endlessly, a cruel taunt teasing us with the promise of safety just out of reach. But I refuse to let doubt cloud my determination. I am not going to let it win this time. I have made a promise to get us across, and I intend to keep it, no matter the cost.

The branch groans beneath us, its weary protest echoing through the dense forest. It's a warning, a reminder that our time teetering on this precarious limb is rapidly dwindling. Sweat cascades down my spine, each droplet hinting at the flowing river below. My fingers ache with strain, clinging desperately to the rough bark for dear life. In this moment of peril, the pressure of Jess's hands around me is the only lifeline keeping me grounded, anchoring me to maintain focus on what's ahead and not below.

With a final, heart stopping lurch, we propel ourselves forward, our bodies pulling toward the solid ground like magnets. Miraculously, we reach the other side. Solid ground greets us like a long-lost friend, offering sanctuary from the dizzying heights and vertiginous drop below.

I collapse onto the welcoming ground, my limbs trembling with exhaustion and adrenaline. Each breath I draw feels like a precious gift, as if I've been holding it in for an eternity. Beside me, Jess mirrors my descent, her own form shaking with the residual tension of our daring escape.

With a surge of relief so intense it borders on euphoria, I collapse onto solid ground, gasping for breath as if I've been holding it the entire time. Jess follows, her trembling form falling beside me as we both struggle to catch our breath. Breathing in the pumped air has never felt better as the mask works its magic.

"We made it," I say, the words a hoarse whisper of disbelief. "We actually made it." I want to sound more confident, but I can't help myself.

Jess doesn't respond, her expression a mixture of exhaustion and lingering fear. But as I look into her eyes, I see something else there too—a glimmer of passion, a look that I wish I could have taken a photo of and drawn as many times as I possibly could.

As we sit there, catching our breath, I feel like I'm suspended in that moment with Jess. There's a certain electricity in the air, a buzz of emotions that neither of us quite knows how to articulate. I steal a glance at her, finding solace in the familiarity of her presence yet feeling the weight of something unspoken between us.

"We did," Jess finally murmurs, her voice barely above a whisper, yet it echoes through the cavernous space around us. Her eyes meet mine, and for a heartbeat, it feels like the world slows down, like we're the only two people in existence.

I want to say something profound, something that encapsulates everything I'm feeling in that moment. But words fail me, as I still don't fully understand exactly what I feel. So, I settle for a nod, hoping she can decipher the emotions swirling within me as easily as I can see them in her eyes.

And just like that, the moment passes, swallowed up by the enormity of our situation. But even as we push ourselves to our feet to continue on our journey, that brief exchange lingers in the back of my mind, a silent reminder of something unspoken yet palpable between us. I stand up from the dazzling light purple blades, similar to grass, on which we sit and reach my good arm out for her to grab.

"You're something else, JJ." She blinks quickly as she stands in front of me, her gaze never leaving mine as she speaks.

"Are you ready to show me?" I smile with my eyes to show her how much I truly care, not only about finding this secret place but also about her and how much this means to her.

"Follow me." She tosses her hair back behind her shoulders, and we start our way through the strange trees once again.

"Why would I follow you when we can totally do this in a far more fun manner?" I have an idea, but I'm not sure yet if it's Jess-approved.

"What do you want?" Her classic head tilt and raised eyebrow almost make me second-guess asking her, but I know she'll like it if we do it.

"Are you down for a piggyback ride?" I laugh at myself, looking down at the ground and shaking my head before turning my attention back to her response. "Yeah, I totally sound like a three-year-old, don't I?"

"What about your shoulder, idiot?" Ignoring my remarks, she pops her hip out to the side with her hand now firmly on it.

"You know you want to! Plus, you weigh like nothing, come on." I already forget about my aching shoulder; honestly, I don't really care anymore.

"Fine, but not for long. I'm not listening to you complain about hurting if you want to do stupid boy stuff instead of taking it easy." She rolls her eyes, but there's no way she can hide the bits of excitement I see sparkling through her eyes as she gets near.

I bend down and hold my bad arm down and my good arm back to help guide her onto my back. She jumps, and I instantly stumble a bit to catch my balance. Holding onto her leg with one hand is a little more challenging than anticipated, but there's no way I'll tell her that.

Piggyback rides have been our thing since we first started hanging out. I remember the very first time we snuck into the meeting room when it was closed and ran around everywhere, climbing on all the seating and playing tag for hours. It was one of my happiest memories—until, of course, I realized the meeting room had cameras and Dad found out about it.

"Now, lead the way, madame! Your chauffeur is prepared for our journey ahead!" I adjust her position slightly and step forward as her arms gently hug around my neck, ensuring not to put too much weight on my injured side.

She unravels her right arm past my face and straight into the unmarked path ahead, her fingers pointing in the direction she insists we should go.

Chapter Twelve

The Rain

The world around us transforms as we venture deeper into the unfamiliar landscape. Strange plants with shades of iridescent blues and shimmering greens line our path, their leaves whispering secrets as we pass. Each step brings us closer to the unknown, and yet, with Jess by my side, I can't help but feel a sense of exhilaration coursing through my veins. As we walk, Jess leads the way with a confidence that hides the uncertainty lurking beneath the surface and the swirling chaos of our lives that led up to this.

The air is alive with the scent of exotic blooms, their perfume mingling with the crisp freshness of the forest. I breathe it in deeply through my mask, allowing the scent to fill my lungs and recharging my spirit. The clearing opens up before us like the pages of a long-forgotten fairy tale. Bright light rays filter through the canopy above, casting a golden hue over the landscape and illuminating the towering figure that stands at its center.

And there it is, a marvel of nature unlike anything I have ever encountered. The branches rise from the center of the earth like a titan reaching for the heavens. Its trunk spirals upward, each curve different than the next. It is as if the tree itself is alive, stretching outwards in a symphony of movement that defies logic and reason.

I feel a shiver of awe course through me as I take in the sight before us, my breath catching in my throat at the sheer magnitude of it all. For a moment, I am transfixed, lost in the wonder of the world still unfolding around me.

"This is it," Jess whispers, her voice barely more than a breath against the stillness of the forest. "This is the Caddell you've always needed to see, yet no one ever even knew it was here." She slides off my back and makes her way next to me.

Her words snap me out of my reverie, and I turn to look at her, the intensity of her gaze mirrored in my own. There is a new tint in her voice, a deep appreciation showing through for the beauty that grows majestically in front of us. Together, we approach the base of the tree, our footsteps echoing softly against the forest floor. The space around us is alive with the consistent hum of the lights and the bustle of the plants, but beneath it all is a sense of stillness, a quiet calm that seems to permeate the very air we breathe.

I reach out a hand, hesitating for just a moment before allowing my fingers to brush against the smooth bark of the monstrous organism. It is cool to the touch, the surface worn smooth by centuries of wind and rain. I trace the intricate patterns etched into its surface, my mind swimming with questions and wonderings about the secrets it holds.

My voice finally speaks softly and cracks slightly without me wanting it to. "It's unlike anything I've ever seen before."

Jess nods beside me, her eyes shining with a mixture of excitement and awe. "I know," she says, her voice barely more than a whisper. "It's like something out of a dream."

Standing here beneath the towering branches of the tree, I can't shake the feeling that we have stumbled upon something truly magical, a place where time stands still and the boundaries between reality and fantasy blur into one. It seems too good to be true, something beyond imagination.

"Isn't it incredible?" Jess asks, her eyes shining with unbridled enthusiasm.

I can only nod, my throat tight with emotion. This is more than just a plant; it is a symbol of everything we have endured, a testament to the strength of our bond. Something Jess has waited all this time just to show me.

The canopy of the tree shades the ground where we stand, creating a shimmer over the dancing plants beneath our feet and allowing us to view the tree's remarkable beauty more clearly. "Are you up for a climb?" She turns to me as we touch the soft bark. How could I ever say no to her daring tone? Even though I am weak from carrying her here, I don't want to let her see a weaker version of me now.

I hesitate before I answer and rub my hand slowly against the tree, giving the impression of uncertainty for a split second before patting the wood twice and hopping onto the first limb. "I'm so in." I turn to her and reach my arm out, just for her to shake her head and giggle before swatting at my leg and climbing up herself.

"Bet, race you to the top then, Mr. One-Arm." She starts to jump and reach her way higher past me and up the tree. There is no way in heck I am going to let her win, one-armed or not. "You got yourself a deal then, Jessica!" I holler back up at her and climb carefully to the second limb. The pain isn't as bad anymore, but one wrong move could cause it to tear through me once again. I try not to think about it as I attempt to move as quickly as I can.

Our voices echo through the world that fades slowly below us.

"I know I will beat you, slowpoke!" she yells down at me from the top branch. "But seriously, dude, you have got to see this!"

It is more work than anticipated trying to climb a massive staircase of winding branches. I try to move quickly, but my efforts slow me down more as my arm throbs with each pounding step I take upward.

"Haha, so funny," I say through shortened breaths. "Fine, you win. What do I owe you?"

"Just hurry up, would you!" she screams back, ignoring my question entirely.

I climb a few more notches of branches until I am able to see her bright hair glowing in the light it's catching from above. I make my way to the top of the tree's overwhelmingly large canopy and find Jess, her sight set on the horizon ahead.

I adjust myself until I am standing directly in line next to her, taking in every bit of what she is seeing. It has to be miles and miles of land that seem to have no end. There are no walls or borders, just so much space left unexplored. We are so high that all the trees, which had seemed fairly large when we stepped over their sideways trunks earlier, are nothing but small dots among the vast surroundings.

"This is it, this is what I want to show you," she says, keeping her eyes on the world that consumes us.

I am amazed, truly. The colors of the plants below, of every color and shade, twinkle with each speck of light that touches their reflecting leaves. The way the world seems to go on and on, and no matter which way you look, everything is so new. The view is stunning, and as much as I want to keep looking out, the most gorgeous view I could ever see is standing right here beside me. She is so fascinated by the shimmering specks below, her eyes filled with such a beautiful spark of passion and happiness. This is it, this is my moment.

The moment I have waited my entire life for.

I swallow harder and more loudly than I probably should. My hands start to sweat slightly, and my thoughts race around in circles about how I am going to say this to her. I shuffle myself slightly closer to her and clear my throat. I finally get her to turn toward me for the first time since we made it to the top. I feel my heart pounding violently as it tries to escape the cage it is trapped in. It's on the tip of my tongue. I am just about to start saying it, to say everything I have kept within me for so long.

Jess breaks the silence before I can get my words together, her voice barely audible yet carrying a weight that seems to press against my chest. "You know, I never imagined that it could be this lonely here." I turn to her, my hazel eyes shimmering with a mixture of vulnerability and longing.

"Lonely," I echo, the word hanging in the air like a poignant melody. "But not entirely. I mean, you've got me here, right?"

My soft, smirky smile glows back at her through my expression above my mask. She sighs, a small, wistful sound that seems to carry all the unspoken words between us.

"Yeah, I guess so," she says, her eyes searching mine as if trying to find something hidden within them. "But it's different. Even with you here, it feels like there's this... emptiness."

I reach out, my worn hand gently brushing against her arm. "Maybe that's just how it is when things change," I suggest, my voice tender. "We're not used to it yet. It takes time to adjust."

Jess nods slightly, her eyes fixed on the ground as if searching for words engraved in the wood. "Yeah, you're here," she acknowledges quietly, her voice tinged with a hint of uncertainty. "But someti mes... it still feels like I'm alone in my own head, you know?"

Her admission strikes a chord within me, resonating with my own struggles in ways I haven't fully realized until this moment. "I get it," I murmur, reaching out tentatively to rest a hand on her shoulder. "I've been so caught up in my own darkness that I never stopped to think about yours."

Jess flinches at my touch, a reflex born from years of guarding herself against pain. But then, to my surprise, she leans into my touch ever so slightly, her shoulder softening under my hand.

"It's okay," she whispers, her voice barely audible above the rustle of leaves in the gentle breeze. "I never really let anyone in before anyway."

A pang of guilt twists in my chest, realizing just how much she has silently endured while I was drowning in my own turmoil. "I'm sorry, Jess," I breathe, my voice thick with emotion. "I should've been there for you, like you've always been there for me."

Her gaze flickers up to meet mine, and for the first time, I see a glimmer of something raw and unguarded in her eyes. "You were," she says softly, her voice catching in her throat. "In your own way, you were."

Jess looks up at me, her expression softening. "Do you really think we can do this?" she asks, her voice a fragile whisper.

"I know we can," I reply, my gaze steady and unwavering. "We've come this far, haven't we? And we've done it together. I mean, we truly are the last two people left in the world. If anyone has taught me that no matter what, we'll be okay in this mess of a life we're living, it's you."

Her eyes curve into a faint smile, the first genuine one I've seen in days. "You're right," she admits. "I guess I just needed to hear it from you."

I squeeze her arm gently, feeling a spark of connection between us. "And I'll keep reminding you, as many times as you need," I promise.

She takes a deep breath, her shoulders relaxing slightly. "Thank you," she says softly. "For being here. For everything."

"No need to thank me," I say, my voice filled with warmth. "Just promise me you'll keep holding on, and so will I. We'll get through this together, we always do."

Jess nods, her eyes shining with newfound determination. "I promise," she says, her voice steady. In that moment, as we stand together in the quiet stillness, it feels as though the world around us fades away, leaving only the bond between us. The loneliness that seemed so overwhelming begins to dissipate, replaced by a sense of hope and resilience. We are not alone. We have each other, and that is enough.

That's everything.

As we close the distance between us, our boots sinking softly into the damp ground, it feels as though we are navigating through a vast expanse of space, traversing the uncharted territory of our emotions. Just as the gap between us lessens, something extraordinary happens, beyond anything I have ever dreamed of.

It begins to rain in Caddell.

Chapter Thirteen

Just Water

The drips begin to fall from above, at first a gentle drizzle, then gradually gaining intensity until they envelop us in a shimmering veil of droplets. The landscape around us seems to awaken, the rhythmic dance of raindrops transforming the alien terrain into a living, breathing entity. Jess and I stand upon the treetop, our silhouettes etched against the backdrop of a vibrant world now painted in shades of gray.

We spin and look around, and together we scan the horizon through misty vision.

"There's no way! It's raining, James! Oh my gosh! It's actually raining!" I hear her voice clearly, yet it's distanced for a moment in my mind as my priority remains in my sight. She's jumping, happy, and tugging at my side, begging to share this extraordinary response with me.

"Look! It's so amazing! I can't believe this is really happening! James, it's... James?" Her voice trails off, and I feel her energy drop as she notices my nearly numb expression as I stand still, my gaze set far ahead.

I wish I could explain it to her, how beyond compare this moment is for me. I've spent my entire life in a house that was never a home, not understanding who I am or even my own name, growing up without knowing what it's like to have someone that needs you in return. I've spent every single day running from myself in my mind, searching for an answer that would somehow fix every part of me that is broken.

For the first time in my life, I feel as though I've finally made it.

I found my answer.

My hand moves to my oxygen mask, my fingers deftly unclasping it with a steady motion. Panic surges within Jess as she watches, her voice trembling with fear and urgency.

"What are you doing!" she exclaims, her words laced with concern. "Do you have a death wish or something? That's not funny, James, come on, put it back on—" My resolve is unwavering, my gaze steady as I meet her eyes.

"I want to feel the rain," I declare.

My voice carries a mix of determination and vulnerability that seems to leave Jess momentarily speechless. I see her watching, breathless, as my oxygen alarm begins to sound. I don't even flinch. I don't care. I take off each latch and release every suctioned area that remains attached to the thin skin on my face and around my ears. Instantly, I feel the weight of the mask falling into my palm, my mouth feeling the space around me for the first time in years.

With some force, I keep my eyes locked on Jess as I unclip each tube from the mask and allow my arm to lower with the free-moving mask I now hold solitary. There is a faint thump, barely even heard, as the mask gently leaves my fingers and lands on the wooden ground next to me. I am finally experiencing the sensation of rain against my skin after years of longing.

It is like a scene from a movie as I watch her eyes search every inch of my face structure. We have only ever seen each other the day I arrived here. From that point forward, the way we have looked is only a memory. As we age, our brains create the image we have only thought we would look like now. I am not sure if I am the same person to her as she recalls after all of this time. I know that no matter how I dream Jess looks beneath the boundaries that stay attached, she can only become more beautiful in my eyes.

With audacity coursing through me, I look up from her wandering gaze and welcome the rain, letting it wash over me as if seeking solace in its embrace. It's just water, but it feels as though it's leaving imprints on my bare skin. Each droplet glistens like liquid diamonds on the pale exposed fragments of my body, tracing paths down my neck and disappearing into the folds of my suit. There are no chains holding me down anymore. No voices screaming orders and pressing into my head to tell me I am worthless and force me to believe that. This is my choice, my moment.

As my eyes return to Jess's, I note a further captivating allure about her, a vibrancy that transcends the constraints of our circumstances. For an instant, we both seem to forget the protocols and dangers that loom, swept away by the raw essence of our connection, washed clean by the rain.

Her heart swells with a mixture of fear and admiration as she watches me, my breath catching in my throat. In that moment, she stands still as she watches me for the first time, looking so utterly alive, that she can't help but feel a surge of something akin to awe. I shatter the constraints of our reality, daring to defy the boundaries that confine us to the unforgiving expanse of the world we stand within.

After a tense pause, she makes her decision. With trembling hands, she follows suit, removing her own face wear. The cool droplets instantly mingle with her hair, sending shivers down her spine as I watch her.

Everything about her is so perfect, her nose so symmetrical, and her soft cheeks holding a slightly pink glow. Her chin and jawline are pristine, a face of a model left hidden for so long. Her lips are the most natural, calming shade that I can't help but spend a few more moments dwelling on. Even if I still had my mask on, I don't think it's possible to breathe anyway as I drink in her smooth skin, my view following the rain as it makes its way to new territory. Soon, I find myself focusing on one particular drop of water as it begins moving down her.

As the raindrop traverses the landscape of her soft skin, it encounters the gentle curve of her cheekbone, gliding delicately along the surface like a miniature skater on a frozen pond. Each contour it navigates seems purposefully carved by a master sculptor, accentuating her beauty in ways that words fail to capture.

Descending further, the raindrop encounters the slight rise of her cheek, where it pauses momentarily, as if savoring the moment before continuing its journey. With each passing second, it leaves behind a trail of glistening evidence.

From there, the raindrop reaches the edge of her jawline, where it hesitates, as if reluctant to depart from such hallowed ground. But even the most reluctant traveler must eventually continue its voyage, and so the raindrop complies, tracing the elegant curve of her jaw with the grace of a dancer performing a final bow.

Finally, as the raindrop reaches the tip of her chin, it lingers for a heartbeat, as if reluctant to depart from this paradise it has found. But with a silent sigh, it releases its grasp, spiraling downward in a final descent, leaving behind only the memory of its fleeting touch on her flawless canvas.

The rain intensifies, surrounding us in a watery embrace. It all feels like a dream. Each droplet feels like a gentle caress against my skin, a reminder of the fragile beauty of existence in this foreign world. And as I meet her gaze, I know that I am exactly where I am meant to be.

In the midst of the rain-soaked landscape, our eyes lock, and it feels as though time itself has come to a standstill. I close the distance between us, my movements deliberate yet filled with an urgency that mirrors the vast variation of emotions within me. With each step, I draw nearer to her, until there is barely a breath of space between us.

"I never thought I'd find something so beautiful in this unforgiving world," I confess, my voice carrying the weight of a thousand unspoken truths through a faint voice, careful not to expand my held breath too far. Jess's eyes brim with unshed tears, her gaze locked with mine in a silent communion that transcends words.

"Maybe beauty is what we make of it," she replies, her voice a whisper against the backdrop of rain. Her bottom lip quivers in the cold air.

My fixated focus watches each drop as they run down her. Though the exchange of air was forbidden, our trade of lust was inevitable. The raindrops dance around us, a symphony of emotions echoing the pounding of our hearts. It was as if the world had faded into the background, leaving only the two of us suspended in the moment.

Despite my fears, I lean in closer quickly, my heart pounding in my chest. Her eyes widen slightly, but she doesn't move away. I'm scared. I don't know how to kiss.

What if I can't do it?

Just as I'm about to pull back, doubting myself again, she closes the gap. Her soft lips meet mine, instantly showing me that I can.

Butterflies are flapping their wings hysterically through my torso as her lips meet mine, her touch sending sparks of electricity coursing through my veins. It was a feeling I had long denied myself, buried beneath layers of duty and responsibility. But in this moment, with the rain caressing my skin and her presence engulfing my senses, I allowed myself to surrender.

As we pulled away, our breath mingling with the rain-soaked air, I found myself lost in her gaze. Her eyes, usually filled with a playful glint, now held a depth I had never seen before. Just like me, she has been broken for so long, and it's almost as if, in just this one moment, all of our shattered pieces have been sealed back together.

We stood there, our hearts interlocked amidst the rain-soaked landscape, our confession sealed in the embrace of the world we had made into our own. I leaned in for just a few seconds more, holding my breath as our lips touched once again. I closed my eyes and allowed myself to take in this memory to replay forever.

As our oxygen alarms blared and we began to pull apart, I kept my eyes shut for just a few seconds more. My cheeks were flushed red from the events that had just taken place. I felt myself smile bigger than ever before, and I knew she had to be smiling too, at the sight of me sharing my smile for the first time in so long. I squeezed my eyes shut tight at the feeling one last time. I couldn't stop myself from grinning.

I felt a single tear form and fall from my closed eyes as we kissed. Men don't cry, but boys do. I am still a boy at heart, a boy who never knew what love was until now. My chest started hurting from the lack of oxygen, and I knew it was time to break our soft, connected touch and come back to reality.

I opened my eyes, expecting to see her pretty face looking back at me, the same pink cheeks as mine and a slight smile she would try to hide. Only, it's nothing like I expected. Just as quickly as they came, the butterflies all flew away in every direction. I was instead met with a wash of panic. I looked for something, anything. But there was nothing beyond the neatly placed mask looking back at me instead of those amber eyes, and a puddle of just water where she had stood.

Jess is gone.

Chapter Fourteen

Mr. Dark

I scream, but my voice is broken by the sharp pins of needles, with no clear air filling my lungs. I need to go, I need to find her. I need to help her. But I can't do any of that without getting air into my lungs first.

Frantically, I throw myself onto the hard surface of the thick branch, using both arms to untangle the heap of machinery and attach it to myself. Everything tingles, and I need to gasp for air, but I fight everything within me not to. One, just one breath of too much of the Caddell atmosphere could cost me my life.

Before I can even attach the plates to my chest, I secure my face mask and begin inhaling into the device. I am desperate, and inhaling that fresh air into my body has never felt better.

Except for the fact that Jess is still somewhere without it.

The tubes are knotted but still functioning, and I can't even think about making sure everything is attached to me properly. I run and slide over to the edge, pacing around, screaming for her.

“Jess! Jess, where are you? Jess!” My voice cracks with anxiety and fear, and adrenaline rushes through every vein in my sore body. The feeling of a rock rolling around in my chest grows heavier with each second that passes, and in between my cries for her, the silent return keeps pushing it deeper into me.

"Jess! Oh God, Jess, please, where are you? Help! God, someone help me!" I don’t even know why I thought yelling for help would do any good. We are alone.

I am alone.

I do the only thing I can possibly do. I grab her oxygen equipment and hustle as quickly as I can back down the tree. I slide my way down the area we shot up to reach the top and scan around at ground level as I leap. I am always a bit scared of heights—heck, what am I not scared of? None of that matters, though. Not right now.

Nothing matters more than Jess.

"Jess! Jess!" I am out of breath. My oxygen plates make sure to keep informing me of that with their forever annoying beep as I cut my air into short gasps, moving far too quickly with one arm down the trunk. Still, there is no voice coming back to me.

I stop halfway, not because I want to, but because if I don’t, I fear I will pass out, and then I will never be able to find her. I stop, my one functioning arm propped against the bark as I inhale and exhale assertively. I have a much better view of the ground now, and I elect to use this brief recovery time to keep searching.

My body is shaking, and my mind won’t stop twisting in every direction. My eyes bounce across the purple-hued plants shimmering and reflecting off the light rays, making it hard to find the little details and objects hidden in it.

"Jess! Please, oh God, where are you? Jess!" My breathing slows, and I start to make my way back down when I see the shaded, dark area in the plants near the spot where we had been standing way above. I know it's her.

I stumble, my leg catching on a smaller branch, sending me down faster than anticipated. Instinctively, I reach my bad arm out to catch myself, pushing my shoulder in with pressure and sending the most stabbing pain imaginable through my chest and entire right side. I grunt and yell out, but I have to keep going. My pain means nothing compared to what Jess means to me. I feel like I am flying, the thought of Jess lying there, still and unmoving, pulsing down my spine. I ignore my pain, my suffering, all to get to her.

My feet land hard as I jump from the ground as soon as I can, and I run to the flattened area in the plants where I see her lying. My heart feels like it could shoot straight out of me, and yet I still don't think I can stop running.

As soon as I get there, I collapse over her. There she lies, my beautiful, funny, always-there-for-me Jess. I feel over her face and her arms and place my two fingers on her neck, praying, wishing, waiting for a pulse to thump against my shaking fingertips. It's all too calm, and only a faint rhythm is left to meet mine.

I fumble like I always do, but in a far more unstable pattern. I can't cry or do anything. I feel so numb, so useless. She is dying. Jess is dying.

I do everything I can think of. I unravel her oxygen from my arm, only to realize it has broken during my climb down. The left tube attachment clamp has a clean crack where light can be seen straight through. If only I still had my one extra tube, but instead, I was too selfish at the time to get a new one after I broke it by making dumb decisions, like I always do.

"Jess, please, you're going to be okay! Please stay, Jess, please! I'm here, I'm right here!"

Her lips are turning shades beyond the faint red they had been just a moment ago, a slim blue making its way through. She's fallen from too high, her body still and unable to move.

"Jess, please wake up, please, Jess!" I am delusional, caught in another realm that feels like a dream, a nightmare. Something no one expects, something people choose to avoid even imagining.

I don't know what to do. She is the one trained for medical help. She is the one who would know what to do, not me. She is the one who saves me, not the other way around.

My thoughts trail away as I break, her body already starting to feel cold as I place my hands over her cheeks, shaking her slightly in hopes that somehow she will answer, that she will be okay. Jess saves me, she saves me. And now I'm the one sitting here watching her die.

"Wake up, come on Jess, please! Dang it, Jess, wake up!" I feel so limp, so painfully numb. I am just sitting here, watching my best friend die in front of me, and there is nothing I can do.

Suddenly, her gasps ring through my head, a slim sign of hope. She coughs, grabbing the ground around her as she pleads for air.

Her eyes are looking around frantically before focusing on me, a look I never wanted to imagine.

"Jess, please, how do I help you? What can I do... Jess, I don't know what to do!" My chest hurts with the unbearable will to do something but being left with nothing.

"Don't do this to me, Jess, not now. I'm not ready... Jess, I'm not ready. You can't leave me here, Jess, please, please, please, Jess!"

I kneel down beside her in an attempt to pick up her head and shoulders. I prop her up on my lap as I cry. The tears sprinkle over her face and down her limp body. I cough and gasp as the crying makes it hard to breathe myself, but I don't care.

I watch her scared face somehow turn soft as a tear forms in both her eyes, a single drop rolling from each of them nearly at the exact same time. I wrap my hand around her head, my thumb rubbing her soft cheek and wiping the left tear away in the process. It's as if the world around me is dimming, the sounds are all muffled.

Every detail, every aspect of her expression, her touch, feels heightened, almost surreal. Her skin feels so cold against mine, projecting a sense of unease that grips me. She doesn't have a single scratch or bruise; she's not bleeding anywhere. She is just lying here so peacefully, as if she's sleeping. Why me? Why Jess? Why *us*?

I yell into the stagnant air, breaking with every breath I have that she doesn't. As I brush her cheek, feeling the dampness of her tears against my thumb, I start to see how blind I've been. How could I have missed the signs of her pain? All of the silent cries for help masked behind her smiles consume my staggered thoughts.

Guilt washes over me, heavy and suffocating, as I realize the depth of her suffering, the weight she's been carrying alone. She's right, even at this dire moment, I'm consumed with yet another conversation with another part of myself trying to find any reason for this not to actually be happening, but it's no use.

She is the one hurting. She is in so much pain, and I can't bear seeing her like this. I want to go back, take away every moment I complained about my problems to her. Nothing can compare to this. All this time, all the hurt she is in, and I have been too self-absorbed to see it.

Yet, she is the one dying, and I am still here.

"Jess, I... I'm so sorry," my voice chips away as I reach her hand up and press my face into her cold palm. I break into a hundred little pieces, falling between her fingertips as my own stream of tears falls onto her.

"JJ..." Her voice, with nothing more than a crackle in her throat, speaks to me.

I jump back, my blurry, wet vision searching for her expression. I am instantly met with her smile looking back at me, though her eyes are becoming hazy. She then cracks her closing mouth once again, and I lean in close to hear even the slightest hint of a voice left in her.

"Don't... blame... yourself," she squeezes out, barely getting any pronunciation on the Y in "yourself." Even in her hardest times, she always puts me above herself.

I can't get any more words out. All I can do is smile back at her for the last time as we both die while witnessing her leave. With her hand on my cheek still, I feel the faintest tug of her thumb, an attempt to wipe the tear off my face. I cry harder into her, placing her limp hand over my mask and mouth.

I see the last look she still holds in her eyes as her smile slowly fades but is still there through it all. She wants to say that it is all going to be okay, I can tell. Seeing me broken, I think truly hurts her more than it could hurt me. I gently move the hair away from her eyes and feel for a pulse down her neck once again.

"Please, please stay—" My words are cut short by the rock I hold in my chest falling into me and crushing everything. The faint, yet consistent pounding in her chest has stopped. Seconds pass, and still nothing.

I lean over her, screaming out and sobbing, holding her closer than I ever have before.

"God, I can't live without you, Jess, please come back!" I yell into the abyss of still life surrounding us.

None of it seems like it's actually happening; the regular debates in my mind circle around me. It can't be happening; this is impossible. Jess can't die, but she is. I cry through a crackling, heartbroken tone. I have nothing left. She is my almost nothing, the one reason, my reason for still smiling, for still pushing forward, for still being myself. She is my reason for still living.

I feel like I do so many things wrong in my life without even meaning to, like I am born to be someone that everyone steps on, that everyone looks through. I am born to be a shadow, a nobody in a world of somebodies. When I have nothing, Jess is there. When I am at my lowest, Jess is there. When I smile, Jess is the only one who sees, who truly admires me for who I am, Caddell or not. She loves me for being just James. Jess saves me in every way that a person can be saved.

I pull my thoughts slightly together as I look down at her, so peacefully laying. She is an angel in my eyes, and one that has gained her wings far too soon. I can't let that happen. I have to bring her back down before she gets too high.

"My sweet Jess—" I slip, and a loud, gasping cry clips through as I try to contain my emotions enough to speak. I don't know what to do now; all I know is that there is no way for me to go on like this without her.

"It is my turn to save you now."

My eyes shine down at her through my foggy vision. If there is one thing I am doing right in my life, it's this. I bring her close and let her lean against my leg as I begin to unclasp my oxygen system. The alarms instantly start again, but I choose to think they aren't there.

Through everything, all the times I feel so meaningless in this world, I feel like I am making the best decision I have ever made. I can't live without Jess, but I know more than anything that she is strong and can achieve more in this life than I ever will. I want to dwell on my actions, taking each piece of my equipment and fastening it firmly onto her still, motionless self before me. But instead, I remain focused on saving her in the last way I know possible.

I hold my breath for as long as I can, though the seconds feel like minutes and I need to let go. Once she is secured, I watch as the system begins to function, moving in and out the toxic gases and filling her with new, fresh oxygen. I cry as I watch, holding back every single drop of strength not to inhale as I watch the machine do its job.

I allow myself to fall to the ground, my body suddenly feeling so much heavier. There, I lie beside her, watching the oxygen fill her lungs and hoping it's enough to bring her back. The seconds keep counting, the mask keeps filtering.

But Jess stays still.

My shaking limbs grow slowly still, and the grip I hold tightly with my other hand on my plate begins to loosen until I let it fall away. I don't know if I will be given a death filled with happiness like most, but that's okay, I guess. I don't want to die like most; I am far from most. All I care about is her; all of my happiness is because of Jess. I love her, and maybe one day, somewhere far from here, I will be able to finally tell her that.

I don't have the strength to sit back up; there's only one more thing I can do now. With a slow and shaking hand, I feel around on the ground below until I find her soft skin against mine. The tips of my fingers trace up her unmoving palm, pushing further towards the grooves between her fingers. My eyes are closed as I take in as much as I can, drinking in the feeling of her touch.

"Thank you," I whisper softly to her through empty lungs. Here we rest as the final two people on Earth, lying together and holding hands for both the first time—and the last.

I take in one final breath, the gases filling my body and replacing every crevice within. They say that in your last moments, you are overcome by your happiest memories. You're filled with happiness once again by those you were happiest with. I am so scared, and I don't want to stop, but as much as I try, I can't force my shutting-down body to draw in another gasp of air beyond that.

I don't know if it's what the foreign air is now doing to my mind or if maybe this is actually happening. Her body begins to dissolve into a million little particles floating away. Each and every piece of her is leaving me. I wave my fingertips out, but I'm met with nothing but the strange-textured plants beneath us.

Through my blurred vision, I see myself too starting to disappear into the air. I know the pain is only temporary, and soon it will all be gone. The dark starts to feel like the best place to be now, and I know that nothing I do can stop it from consuming me. I wish we had more time, a few more minutes spent together. But living is a choice we never got to make, and death must be the same.

Instead of turning and running away like I always have, I decide to stay. When I was a kid, I had a figure in my head nicknamed Mr. Dark, who only came out when he knew I was in a weak or vulnerable state. He always said he wanted to take me away from here, mainly at times when my dad would cause me the deepest pain. I was too scared of him to ever go near him, even when I knew he was just trying to set me free from my hurt.

This time, though, when Mr. Dark reaches out his hand, I finally let his grip match firmly with mine and allow him to take me with him.

Chapter Fifteen

The Waving Shadow

It is calm, and all of my pain has gone away now. I feel my grasp fading until I feel like I am floating, like I am in space. The particles I see of me and Jess are spreading everywhere into the dark background. It doesn't take me long to realize that the tiny flakes are turning into stars. I am an astronaut, just like I have always dreamed of. Only, I have no equipment. I am just endlessly spinning through the newly twinkling stars.

It is everything I imagined at first, but then, for some reason, a wash of concern spreads through me. If I am in space, then I need air. Glancing down, I notice I have no suit, no helmet, and no oxygen pack. I am lost, and my airway begins to tighten as I try to breathe with nothing in return.

I begin to gasp and cough, holding my throat as I drift, wanting to scream, but my voice is muted. I jolt myself around, trying to get air, fear radiating through me. But, all at the same time, I am numb. I feel myself slipping further away. My own lungs are collapsing as the still air provides no source of life. Almost as quickly as they had gone just moments ago, I can hear the familiar sound of the oxygen monitor crying out hysterically once again.

The world is black and fuzzy as I begin to resume my focus. My chest hurts from breathing so fast and hard. At first, I think it is Jess again, and for a second, I am thankful my mask worked on her enough for her to attempt to save me too, as irrational as that sounds. Just a glimpse of a person, a ghostly figure my brain makes me believe is real.

There is a mask back on my face, and my shoulder burns now with an even hotter flame of pain than before. It takes me only a few seconds to realize everything. It is all dark surrounding me once again, and I am sitting against something solid holding up my back. Everything is black except for a single glow torch flickering just a few feet away from me.

I shudder, kicking my feet as I start to consume everything that is actually happening. I watched Jess leaving as I held her in my arms. I know that what I saw and what I heard is real. We just spent the best moments of our lives together: the magical tree, the rain, and the close distance between us. The conversations, sleeping in the bed together, crossing the branch, and laying in the flowers. Using what I could in a final attempt to save her life, giving up my last breath for hers.

Yet, none of that *actually* happened.

I've been trapped in my own mind, lost in delusions and hallucinations. I should have known; there were so many signs that I just chose to ignore. I knew it had to be too good to be true.

Freedom doesn't exist for someone like me, and neither does love, apparently.

The fear holds me tightly as I struggle to distinguish between what is real and what is merely a creation of my own. Grabbing control of something closer to full consciousness, the questions start rolling in. I slowly begin to observe what is actually happening. I look down at myself first. My arm is still cut, though not as badly as I originally thought in the panic of the moment that landed me in this situation.

Blood is still dripping through, forming a growing puddle that I am sitting in. The torch's UV light is the only thing keeping me alive still; it's the only way my suit could possibly still be functioning after as long as I've likely been sitting here. With that, an entirely new wave of panic evolves every time a new branch of reality expands.

How long have I been here?

Upon further inspection, I reach over to my oxygen plate. As expected, the plate is perfectly intact. Oxygen is filling my body just as it always has, with no apparent damage. I'm still here, in the same miserable version of the very place I had finally escaped. The shock made me see things that were never even here.

Jess was *never* here.

My head throbs with a fierce headache that rules over me, and the pain in my arm is horrendous. I have gotten so used to the comfort I had while Jess took care of me in my false reality. None of it happened: the power coming back on, Jess stitching my arm, and spending the time together we always dreamed of. It was all just another dream in my broken mind. But if it isn't real, then where actually is Jess?

Where is *everyone*?

Shifting even slightly into anything close to an upright position hurts everywhere. The bleeding worsens with any movement. My back is sore from the hard stump against which I have been glued for who knows how long. I rub my eyes as I lean forward, stretching with extreme caution. It is so dark, and I just barely manage to use my strong arm to reach the glow torch.

I pick it up and wave it around, taking in the full view of my surroundings. Caddell, our once vibrant home, now lies in ruins. It is so silent and empty. The memories of happier times haunt me, taunting me with what once was and what can never be again. The realization that there is no life left hits me like a sledgehammer, stealing the last remnants of hope from my shattered soul.

My best friend is gone; everything I once knew is gone. I bury my face in my hands, trying to shield myself from the harsh reality of my situation. The weight of grief presses down on me, threatening to crush me beneath its relentless force.

The instincts scream at me to get up, while the voices insist that I stay.

Lifting my head back up, the tears still stream down my cheeks as I wipe my eyes with trembling hands. Anger simmers beneath the surface, fueled by the insanity of it all. Having no choice, I begin to search for something, anything left within this lonely place where I sit. My eyes feel puffy and sore, and I can't stop sniffling under the weight of everything.

I scream at the top of my lungs into the silent world that encloses me, pouring out everything I have left. I have no idea where to go or what to do. There is absolutely nothing left beyond the chills that the eerie darkness of Caddell holds around me.

Nothing can express what it truly feels like to gain everything you've ever wanted and lose it all at the same time.

Just as I am about to lean back against the tree in an attempt to catch hold of my twisted thoughts, I see the smallest bit of light reflecting off something through the corner of my eye. Thrown into a position that causes its internal matter to spill out onto the now jagged ground we sit on together, my drawstring bag with my sketchbook partially exposed peers back at me through the faint glow.

I scoot on my bottom the best I can until I am finally within arm's reach of the loose strings, pulling it closer to me. I wince, gritting my teeth as the pain pulses through my arm with even the weakest of movements.

Tearing the cloth material of the bag, I make myself a strip capable of tying around my wound. Using my left arm and my mouth, I tug and pull the ends at the same time, clenching my teeth and letting out a moan as the pressure latches on.

I take a second to let the pain settle again and decide to bring the sketchbook to my lap. The second I flip open the leather-textured cover, it gives me a view of pages upon pages filled with black and white blurs. Instantly, as if to punch me harder in my already shattered heart, the first two pages I stop on are the ones I had drawn of Jess.

To the left, a moment I had captured so clearly in my mind. She is sitting in the meeting room, her head resting neatly on her arm as she looks up so gently towards the front of the room. Her gaze is set ahead, and the way her lashes curl upward, along with her raised eyebrows, is something I'll never forget.

The reality of it all makes me want to puke. Instinctively, I run my hand down the page. Though, my unsteady hand accidentally blurs the charcoal lines from behind her ear and down her suit, distorting her features slightly. A tear falls to the page as I peel away my fingers, taking her in for just a second longer. But the longer I look, the more I fall apart.

The more and more I fall into a drive for a touch I know I will likely never feel again.

I slam the book shut harder than I need to, sending a small puff of charcoal powder into the air. The dust turns the cracks in my hand into black grooves of patterns and swirls. I lean my head back against the tree, tears drying as I feel the lump rise and fall in my chest. I need to yell out again, harder and louder than ever, but nothing comes. My voice is mute, and my tears are retained.

When you've lost everything around you, it's easy to start to lose yourself too.

Glaring back at the book now tossed a few feet from me, I take in the eerie surroundings of dark shadows and looming trees. Beneath my mask, I scrunch my nose and violently slap my palm into my forehead as hard as I can. Three times, I slap myself in an effort to bring myself to reality.

Two options lay at the doors of my fate. I can either let the darkness consume the life from my suit, resulting in no oxygen and a long, slow death, or I can get out of here, hoping that there's still someone else alive out there too, maybe even Jess. And if not, I could find the way to the surface and reach up to feel a glimpse of sunlight one last time before I too fall to pieces with everything else around me.

I have to get up.

I look around at the world I have grown to try to love. Everywhere I turn, it's just piles of shattered glass and crumpled leaves. Scanning the ground towards the direction I think I came from, I catch a glimpse of a pattern on the ground in the glow of the torch. Almost as if it can hear my thoughts, the faint footprints from my earlier self coming to this area are still barely visible on the hard ground.

I work my way up, nearly falling over from the dizziness that instantly spins me around like a horse on a lead. I don't even care anymore. There's no me without Jess. I'm not even Just James anymore.

My head grows heavy with the migraine that eats at the walls of my skull. Why, of all people, am I the one still here? Alone, I am the last person alive in this unforgiving world. I guess I never really considered how lonely the last man on Earth must have felt in all those books I read as a kid, yet now I am the one living all those fairy tales at once. Unlike the ones I read, though, something tells me this one will have a much sadder ending.

A rage of emotions surges within me, threatening to overwhelm my fragile resolve. Memories, both bitter and sweet, flood my mind, a complicated battle I constantly face with myself. I stand facing the path, the way out of here. I look down once again, my sketchbook begging for me to bring it with me. I don't want to leave it behind; I've spent years drawing everything in that book.

The longer I stand and stare as I feel the warm blood run down my arm beneath the tourniquet, the sooner I realize that those few happy memories preserved within its pages don't deserve to die with me if that's where this path will lead me.

I hesitate while studying the grooves of my boot print sparkling in the light that flickers in my hand. Closing my eyes, I attempt to grab hold of my racing emotions the best I can. There's only one thing I feel even the slightest bit of confidence about now, and that's this final choice I've devoted myself to taking. If she is still out there, I have to find her. My voice is nothing but a crisp whisper in the silence, giving me the push I need to leave the way I want to, not the way the fear in the back of my mind tells me to.

I glance back, debating one final moment about leaving the book behind. Almost as if something knew I needed a sign, the angle at which I was holding the glow torch began to cast dancing shadows of myself on the dark cover of the sketchbook laying alone on the ground. I reach my other hand up, a sharp pain runs across my chest from the rising of my shoulder. I see my hand meeting the light and creating my own intentional shadow. In unison, I wave my fingers back at myself on the book of everything I am, everything I was, and everything I will be.

"Goodbye, James."

Chapter Sixteen

Up, Up, and Away

Each step gets me further from my past and closer to a new unknown. I am scared, I am hurt, but I keep going. All of my hope is lost, except for the repeating thought that if there is still somewhere beyond this life, I will be able to see Jess again there. The jabbing hurt of the idea of her dying alone tingles within me constantly in the background, making every step forward just that much harder. Maybe I can actually get to tell her the one thing I've always wanted to say to her.

My head just keeps pounding with every inch I close into the darkness, dodging familiar plants and trees that I now recall seeing on my way to the tunnel in the first place. I still wish I had gotten the opportunity to show the glowing lights to her. It is all such a confusing feeling. I already accepted my Jess being gone through the hallucinations; it is as if I am living two different stories at the same time. It is strange knowing she is likely officially gone now, but I still feel like everything I already saw was real, when I know it couldn't have been.

Everything is so lonely inside my mind without her, but all I can do through the ache in my shoulder and the games my mind plays is believe that I have a possibility of seeing her again. If I am still alive, maybe she is too. It is a dangerous mentality that makes me question everything. It may be a one in a trillion chance that she's out there, but that's still a chance.

And those are odds that I'm willing to take.

Swirling. That seems like the best way to describe it. Swirling around like cream stirring into a warm cup of coffee. Dang, it's been so long since I've seen coffee, let alone tasted it. I hate the thought of it; the smell makes me nauseous when Mom has it every morning before taking me to school. I always thought of it as a drink that only grown-ups would like, never expecting to be an official adult myself in just a few more weeks and never getting the chance to even try it. Jess, on the other hand, tells me she always loves coffee, and a part of me dreams of the day I can bring her to the one Mom had always loved to buy her coffee from in the big city. If only she could know how badly I need her with me right now.

With each swinging step I make, I keep staggering a little as I slightly trip on some roots in my path, and the pain from my shoulder causes my balance to slightly alter at times. I never consider what Caddell looks like in the dark. I'm still in such a state of disbelief that I don't really think about it much as I trench forward. The odd-colored leaves and strange towering plants keep providing a unique array of shadows as the light passes through them.

For a second, I could swear I heard something in the wooded region to the left of me, just beyond where the light no longer touches. I stop, holding the torch out to get a better view.

"Hello?" my broken, numbed tone reached out. A part of me stood with a hopeful glint sparking in my eye at the idea of someone else still being here, another person to make the lonely less alone. But after a few seconds of only silence, I figured it had to have just been the shadows and my messed-up imagination.

For as long as I can remember, I've always had conversations in my head. Back and forth, a million times, arguing about everything with myself. I spend so much time thinking about the same exact scenarios over and over again until I can't take it anymore. I think I really am the textbook definition of a broken record. Sometimes, my talks within my head do help some, like passing by time just a bit quicker than always living in the moment.

My prints start to fade, and the ground grows into a more familiar path. The bright lights that were once hung high above are now broken everywhere on the ground. I never thought I would be glad to see those strange little mushrooms again, their little triangular points sparkling in the light of the stick in my hand. The same floor appears as though it will sink with my weight pressing into it, though my boots finding the hard surface is all that I am met with.

Before I know it, I am back facing the daunting view in front of me, the clear joint pathway that unfolds into the doorway to the outer world, away from Caddell. With each step of my forward movement, the massive frame comes closer to me. Still standing tall as if entirely unphased by any destruction that has occurred, the giant door keeps the same feeling it always gives as it looks down at me.

As I approach, I notice the sealed massive door left cracked slightly open, a James-sized space for me to slip out through. Or maybe, just maybe, it is a Jess-sized gap. I really need to stop thinking I have a chance to see her again, but something keeps pulling me back from accepting that she is actually gone. I have to refuse to allow myself to believe in my false hopes any longer.

Caddell never stays open; I don't even know how it could have gotten open again since I came in. There's still no power in here. I edge closer, my heart pounding. I slip my way through, clutching the glow torch like a lifeline. It casts flickering shadows on the walls, barely illuminating the path ahead. Each and every secured door is pried open, their mangled frames bearing silent witness to whatever force has broken in.

My breath quickens with every step, anxiety gnawing at my insides as I venture deeper into the unnerving darkness. Making my way over the patches and piles of sharp metal pieces and debris, I find myself nearly face-planting over something sticking out of the rubble.

"Frick! What the heck is that?" My voice echoes, mildly freaked out by my boot snagging the tip of something in the darkness. As old as I am, I still use words that a middle schooler would use instead of the much harsher alternatives.

I turn quickly around, the torch sparking with my abrupt movements. To my surprise, it isn't a piece of glass or metal, or some creepy figure reaching out to trip me, like my mind instantly thinks of.

It's a book.

I bend down, which feels like bricks being thrown at my right shoulder. Picking up the small booklet, its leather texture and worn pages are more than familiar. I shine the torch over the cover as I open it, and in the process, I notice once more the traces of charcoal still settled on my fingertips where I smudged the drawing of Jess. The pit in my core tightens as I think of her once again at the edge of my touch. It's stupid in all of reality, but seeing the charcoal fingerprints on the first page makes me feel as if a small part of her is still with me.

This is my father's planning journal. He never lets anyone touch it. Well, he never lets anyone near him in general, but he is specifically against the idea of any hands near this book. Or maybe he is just against me coming near his book. Either way, it is very precious to him, and I can't believe it's just lying here on the ground. A wave of reality washes over me once again at the idea of my father leaving behind such an item. They must have been in a great hurry to go somewhere.

But *where*?

I quickly skim through the pages, a final resort for answers before I continue with my mission of trekking through the empty halls. As my thumb moves its way up and each page flickers by, there is nothing that gives me anything besides long math equations and scientific formulas on most of the pages. Though I don't understand most of what it is saying, I decide to take it with me anyway. It only feels conclusive to carry my father's legacy with me, destroying the pages that made him who he was along with the son he left behind if there is no hope left down here.

Making my way through the eerily dark hallways, I look around everywhere for any sign of life. The once-familiar corridors of the underground facility now seem so strangely foreign and menacing, sending an oppressive darkness that swallows even the slightest flicker of my torch.

My footsteps echo, the sound amplified by the capacious facility. The air is stale, carrying a faint, musty odor through my mask that hints at neglect and abandonment. I still wish I could know exactly how long I've been left here alone.

I run my fingers down the wall as I go on. The cool, smooth surface of the concrete is a stark contrast to the warm, throbbing pain in my injured arm. The tight material I fasten around my upper arm seems to still be doing its job, though every time I stumble even slightly, a tiny drop of blood still seeps through the edge, making a faint splatter that bounces an echo as it hits the solid floor below.

The silence is truly deafening, broken only by the faint hum of my own oxygen system doing my breathing for me, though I can tell it is struggling some without sunlight in who knows how long. My light flickers sporadically, casting long, ominous shadows both in front and behind me.

Where are they?

I can't help but expect something, perhaps the lifeless bodies of my fellow inhabitants down here. But instead, I find nothing. It is as if they have vanished into thin air, leaving behind only their abandoned belongings and the lingering echoes of their presence. The emptiness keeps gnawing at my mind.

I slowly step past the open door to my own chamber, the very place I've spent the most time in since I was brought here. I can't help but glance briefly inside, and as soon as I do, a wave of nausea spirals through me.

There is the same bed I've spent every single night in, the now-crooked mirror I had one of my last conversations with Jess about, and buried there in the corner within a pile of debris once used as my nightstand is shattered glass with traces of water reflecting in the dim light of my torch.

Zoron.

I would sound crazy to call a fish my friend, but I'd be lying if I said he wasn't. He was the last piece of the Earth I grew up on that I still had left. Just like me, he tried to live a normal and happy life. Yet, just like me, he too had to suffer from the unforgiving world we were forced to share.

I want to say something, to somehow grieve the loss of my little pal. Though I'm more numb than anything right now, words can't speak enough, and crying can't happen after all tears have been shed.

When you've already lost everything, it's hard to feel something.

Quickly, I run inside the room and throw the covers from my bed, making contact with my tracker once again. In frantic yet precise fashion, I fasten it back to my shoulder and lock it in place.

If anyone is still out there, maybe they will be able to find me before I can find them.

Making my way out of the chamber and closing the door gently behind me, I continue to avert my focus back to the desolate hallway. I move carefully; each empty room I pass by enhances the pit of dread in my stomach. Jess's room is only a few more doors down, but I really don't know if I have the guts to go near it.

I turn a corner, taking the last step in the direction of her chamber with the biggest sense of unease building in me. As I get closer, though, I am forced to come to a sudden halt. My glow torch beam falls upon a familiar door that I never really questioned. It is plain, and nothing hinted at anything significant. It looks like some sort of maintenance closet, and I never thought about it more than that. I tried to go into it one day with the curiosity I had in me, and of course, it was locked.

Now, though, this same door is swung open as if done in a hurry. The crumbled debris is shifted almost in a path from both directions down the halls, as if several people had to have made their way through here. The moment I angle the flame enough to see inside, my jaw is already falling to the floor.

As soon as I place one foot inside, I am greeted by a massive elevator, an engineering marvel in itself. This must be it, the way out. A single elevator designed to travel all 24,500 feet back to Earth's surface.

Hesitantly, I come closer until I'm able to reach my torch around the inside. The cabin is spacious, capable of transporting a large group or a substantial amount of cargo, hinting at the grand vision my dad had when he built this place. The walls are lined with sleek, metallic panels, and a faint hum of machinery vibrates the air, indicating the system's readiness despite its apparent age and circumstances.

Somehow, the power in the elevator is still on. It must be solar-powered by the sun on the surface, harnessing the energy through a network of hidden panels above. I imagine the solar arrays stretching out, capturing sunlight to generate the necessary power for such an immense structure. It is a testament to my dad's forward-thinking and the thoroughness of his design.

This elevator isn't just a way down, it is a lifeline back to the surface. A hidden connection to the world above that we have long forgotten. All this time, the way back up has been here. We pass by this door every single day without any of us knowing. This has to be where they all went, whether they're somehow still alive up there or not.

I step inside, hitting the top of the only two button options available, and the doors slide shut. It feels so strange being in an elevator; I haven't been in one since Mom had a job in California, and we stayed in a hotel for two weeks straight. But that memory quickly fades away as the floor starts to shake, and I feel myself being lifted up.

I don't know what to expect as the walls around me whirl away into a blur while I fly to the top. I can't think; I am so drained and confused. Honestly, if being on the surface will kill me, I'd consider it a blessing at this point. This would be my end; I wouldn't see Jess ever again, not here anyway. I wish I could have been there with her as they must have fled these chambers, the home we've had for so long.

If it wasn't for my dumb mind and the games it plays, then she wouldn't have had to be alone through all of this. I'm trying to push down that thought, but it keeps resurfacing and refuses to leave. It's my fault if she died alone. I should have never gone to Caddell alone.

"Here we go," I whisper, my head low as if speaking to a smaller version of myself. The elevator starts to slow as we reach our destination. It's crazy how it goes on for so long, so high above Caddell. Yet, it is known as the ground for everyone who lives here.

Or rather, *did* live here.

As each foot of space between me and the world I used to know gets smaller, I recall everything I can between then and now. I want more than anything to see the world the way I left it once again, the lights of New York City dazzling against the night sky. But I never even consider the idea of actually leaving behind Caddell. I don't have many friends, or people I truly care about for that matter. But I did have Jess. Saying her name in the past tense makes me nauseous once again.

The machine emits its familiar clinking sound, causing my heart to quicken with anticipation. With each passing moment, the sensation of every feeling possible floods through every vein. The doors part, revealing a sight that strikes me like a bolt of lightning. There stands a door, plain and unassuming, yet it carries an immense weight of significance.

Instantly, a surge of recognition floods my senses, catching me off guard with its intensity. This isn't just any door; it's a portal to memories long buried, emotions deeply entrenched. I've seen it before, but always from the outside, a distant symbol of the world I once knew, now lost to me. I feel like I'm stuck in another level of reality that I don't know if I'll ever be able to actually escape. I reach my hands out, my fingertips so close, yet I can never seem to touch it.

In this fleeting moment, standing before the door that bridges my past and present, I feel a powerful connection, a tether pulling me back to a time when things were simpler, when possibilities stretched out before me like an endless horizon. But intertwined with that nostalgia is the stark reminder of my current reality, of the walls that now confine me, trapping me in a world of limitations.

I take a deep breath. I can't believe I'm here, I can't believe I'm going out. I am back on the surface. Should I be scared, excited, nervous? I have no idea what I'm feeling right now. I know that when I open those doors, it will most likely be nothing but dust. It will not be anything like I remember, and everyone will be gone.

I will be gone.

I've spent my entire life preparing to live as one of the 94 people left alive on Earth. I don't know if I will be gone immediately if I go out there, but there is nothing left for me below anymore. So much time, so much life, is wasted trying to fight against the inevitable.

As I stand here, my hand trembling against the icy metal of the door, a surge of conflicting emotions floods through me. Fear, yes, but also a strange sense of liberation. For so long, I've been imprisoned by the walls of this facility. Rules drilled into me, making me lose my mind further from the person I think of myself as.

But now, as I prepare to step out into the unknown, there is a flicker of hope igniting within me. Perhaps it's the desperate longing for connection, for purpose, that drives me forward. Or maybe it is simply the fact that there really is nothing left to lose.

With a deep breath, I prepare myself the best I can for what lies ahead. Clutching the glow torch and the book close to my chest, their weight a comforting anchor in the uncertainty that surrounds me, I feel a surge of desperation coursing through my veins. This is my moment, my chance to break free from the chains of the past and embrace whatever fate awaits me beyond that door.

Closing my eyes, I whisper a silent prayer to whatever god may still linger in the empty expanse of the world outside. I pray I will see her beautiful face again. Not one hidden behind a mask, nor one pressed with a hurt that fights inside her just as much as mine does. I hope when I go out, I'll somehow be greeted by her presence, no matter how long it may take. With a final, trembling exhale, I count down from three. Each number is a heartbeat echoing in the stillness of the air around me.

Three... Two... One...

Chapter Seventeen

Almost Everything

I hold my breath, my eyes still closed, as the radiant beam of the glow torch is swiftly eclipsed by the brilliance of the sun's rays flooding through the open door, casting a blinding halo of light that envelops the room. It takes several moments for my eyes to acclimate to the sudden change in brightness, each second feeling like an eternity as I blink away the disorientation.

Stepping tentatively beyond the door frame, my feet sink into the soft embrace of the Earth's soil. A surge of emotion wells up within me. This is it—the touch of the real world beneath my feet after years of separation. Every sensation, every sight, is a revelation in itself. The air, once thought to be poisoned beyond repair, now fills my lungs with a sweet, familiar freshness that stirs long-buried memories. Tears well in my eyes as I gaze around, disbelief mingling with overwhelming joy.

I was told that nothing would be left of the surface, that it would be a barren wasteland. Yet here it is, as beautiful and vibrant as I remember from my childhood days, when the world was still innocent and full of wonder. It is a moment of connection—not just with the world around me, but with my own past self, the twelve-year-old boy who was brought here.

I drink in the sight of the lush green grass, the trees swaying gently in the breeze, and the vibrant array of fallen leaves carpeting the ground beneath them. Above, the vast expanse of the blue sky stretches endlessly, with wisps of cottony clouds dancing in a timeless ballet. But amidst this breathtaking tableau of nature's beauty, there it stands, looking back at me. The same chain-link fence that marked the boundary between freedom and captivity all those years ago. Its familiar form serves as a symbolic reminder of the past.

I stand in shock. Nothing has changed. It is all so incredibly similar that it feels as if I never left. I start to freak out again, thinking I must be in another dream. What if I am still sitting in the dark? What if none of this even happened? So many questions flood my mind, yet the longer I look around, the clearer it becomes, and the more I can feel everything around me.

I think it's strange that a destroyed Earth's surface would look this way. There are birds—yes, actual birds—sitting in the tree overhead, making a variety of chirps and noises I want to believe are only in my imagination. My instinctive thought is that I must actually be dead. Though, this is not necessarily the way I pictured my next life.

But the longer I stand here, the clearer things become. Even through the mask, I can smell the tainted earthly scent of grass and soil I had forgotten existed. I was trained, forced, and taught to live inside the Earth because nothing was supposed to remain up here after November. But here I am, and here is the world around me. I stand in shock, unsure of what to think anymore.

I want to believe it's real, that there's something preventing us from living here now—not exactly as Dad expected it to look. No matter what I do, nothing can prepare me for the deeper realizations that keep setting in. Yet, I'm just left standing here alone, dwelling upon it all.

"What...what is going on?" I say out loud, needing to voice something beyond the endless conversations in my head.

I had mentally rehearsed the dramatic moment of dropping my mask in the elevator, dedicating myself to inhaling the dusty air and letting this uninhabitable world take me with it. Instead, I violently rip the mask from my face, yanking the tubes apart and out of the plates on my chest before tossing them as hard as I can with my remaining energy. My lungs are met with the fresh earthly air I've longed for. I'm lost, but something about the sunlight catching my suit and the air I'd nearly forgotten sends a wave of calmness through me.

"What now?" I yell, frustration, hurt, and confusion pouring out of me. He leaves me with nothing but this book. Everything I've known for years is just gone, and he can't even be here to help me. "What do I do?"

Though this is the place I used to love, it feels so foreign, so different. I've forgotten what it's like to live like a normal person here.

I throw myself onto the ground, flopping onto my back into the cool green grass below. I look up at the sky, a blue and cloudy painting above me. The bird on the branch glances down at me before fluttering its wings and taking off into the sky. The sun's rays sliver through the trees, beaming onto my pale skin.

There has to be an answer. I just need to find where to look. I'm still me. He's still in there, I know it. Curious and creative James, now is not the time to be shy. I need you more than ever. I don't know if anyone I know is alive. I don't know where to go. My shoulder aches, needing real medical attention. My heart feels like a million shots have pierced it. My mind remains trapped in a cycle of creating endless predictions about what could have happened, none of which make any sense. There is no logical reasoning for any of this, and I can't help but still blame it all on the evil shell of a man I call Dad.

Having no idea what I should do or where I should go, I decide to open his book again. I start at the beginning and roughly flip through each page one at a time. There has to be an answer somewhere.

I allow the pages to flow through my thumb once again in hopes of an answer, and just as I am about to throw it as far as I can away from me, I feel a slight separation between the pages that is barely even noticeable, which must be how I missed it when I looked through it in the darkness below. Frantically, I flip back through the pages in the area where I know I'll see something stand out beyond the white, crisp paper of strange formulas.

Sure enough, I am right.

As I flip again through the gapped pages, a tightly folded and worn piece of paper falls into my lap. Both curious and desperate, I lunge back into a sitting position here on the grass, the fresh dirt clinging to my suit and boots as I adjust anxiously. Carefully, to ensure I don't break the delicate material, I begin to unfold the forbidden paper.

Admiring every detail as the page begins to unravel, I finish smoothing out each corner. Immediately, I'm entirely intrigued by what this has to be about. Without a second more of hesitation, I rotate it right side up and begin reading the last of what I have left.

Instantly, I launch myself all the way up to a standing position, my head spinning a little as I stand up far too quickly. I face the paper stretched firmly between an unsteady grasp, my heart pounding and my palms sweaty. I have so many questions, so much I need to know, so much I need to understand. This has given me another level of purpose, another reason left to keep going.

Another reason left to *live*.

I start by studying the title at the top of the page: "THE CADDELL PROJECT," a large font screams. Beneath it, a smaller type size entices more adrenaline than that above: "EXPERIMENTAL SUBTERRANEAN LIVING FACILITY."

Frantically, I am forced to start reading every word while racing my own mind as I absorb the labeled sketch drawn out beneath. I run my finger down the page, taking in everything that this means, everything that this changes. The elevator, the title, the pinned locations—all of it is here. This isn't just a drawing.

It's a map.

I trace across from the surface, then down the elevator shaft, stopping where I got on when I left Caddell at a place labeled "Testing Location," before continuing down so much farther. There, near the very bottom of the page, the elevator route finally ends. In a series of what appears to be winding tunnels or hallways, the path eventually ends without any further hints as to what is out there. In the vast, empty space that consumes over half of the map, the single word "Caddell" is handwritten.

I can't hold back my previously dried tears any longer. They run down my face and splatter onto the page, slightly blurring some of the ink together. I just stare as I attempt to absorb everything. This means that all of what we've been through was just an experiment.

I'm an experiment.

Over and over again, my wandering eyes scan the page, each time a different section drawing my attention. As I inhale a long sigh in preparation for all the weight that now lies on my shoulders, I see the faint bit of ink on one of my wet tear patches bleeding through. There has to be more writing; I have to know more. I need a reason why he would do this.

I hold it up to the sky, pleading for more. The sunlight makes a faint glow through the paper where my teardrop had landed. Yet, instead of only being met with the clear beam shining back at me, I see a faint bit of ink on the back of the page bleeding through.

There had to be more writing left on the back of the page. I flip it over, desperate and hungry for a better explanation. This time, I decide to read the few words typed neatly in a paragraph in the center of the page out loud as I take each of them in. I stumble at first, but finally build up the courage to say it to the world around me.

"The date scheduled for transport of the final testing group, The Selected #008, is set for 11.23.2052." I take a moment to process the best I can before proceeding. "On this day, residents of the project will be removed from the Testing Location and taken to the permanent living facility of Caddell. Once the final group has been safely relocated, the Testing Location self-destruction will take place. Project inhabitants will remain enclosed in Caddell, having no further knowledge of surface condition or any other world left beyond that in which they are contained."

I let the map flutter out of my hand and onto the ground below. It rests there, and I feel it nearly glaring through the back of my head as I look back up at the sun. I close my eyes as I absorb the warmth of its forgotten rays and inhale deeply through open lungs.

I allow my head to hang low and my eyes to find the map once again, lying exposed for the world to see on the green grass it's likely never touched. It feels like a ticking time bomb sitting right next to me. With a mix of dread and determination, I bend down and pick it up, my fingers tracing the blurred ink once again.

The entire plan, all of it, is in there, and it's all coming together. We've all been in testing this entire time, and now he has them exactly where he wants them—in the real underground realm of Caddell. Their families, jobs, everything they know is taken from them for nothing. There is no destruction of the surface, there is no reason for us to be stuck beneath the soil. It's all right here, scribbled across his unholy pages.

I am not supposed to be here; I was never supposed to see the surface again. Somewhere, the only family I have known now is still trapped in this never-ending experiment behind my father's grip. I have to show them this map; I have to get them out. I have to bring them home, right?

I have a choice.

I can go back into the haunting doors, walk the halls of the very prison I have finally escaped. I risk never making it out again and being trapped once more in my father's evil embrace.

I made it out; I am free, just as I always wished to be. I can roam the Earth, live the life I have longed for forever. Maybe, just maybe, I can even see my mom again. I can have everything I've ever wanted here.

Well, almost everything.

In what seems to be the same moment of held breath and dire contemplation, my peripheral vision catches the faintest glimpse of distinction. As my eyes leave the paper clutched tightly between my shaking fingers, there lies a sign from someone, somewhere, that there is more for me.

Some may choose to believe that it is just a coincidence, but for me, I know it has to mean something beyond that. It's a light shining through the darkness like it always does, penetrating the deep shades of green that surround. Swaying in the soft breeze, isolated in its contrast to the world around it, yet peaceful in its unique differences. There it is, a sliver of hope amidst my moments of despair.

It doesn't matter anymore if this is real or all in my head. I already have my answer.

A single tiny purple flower.

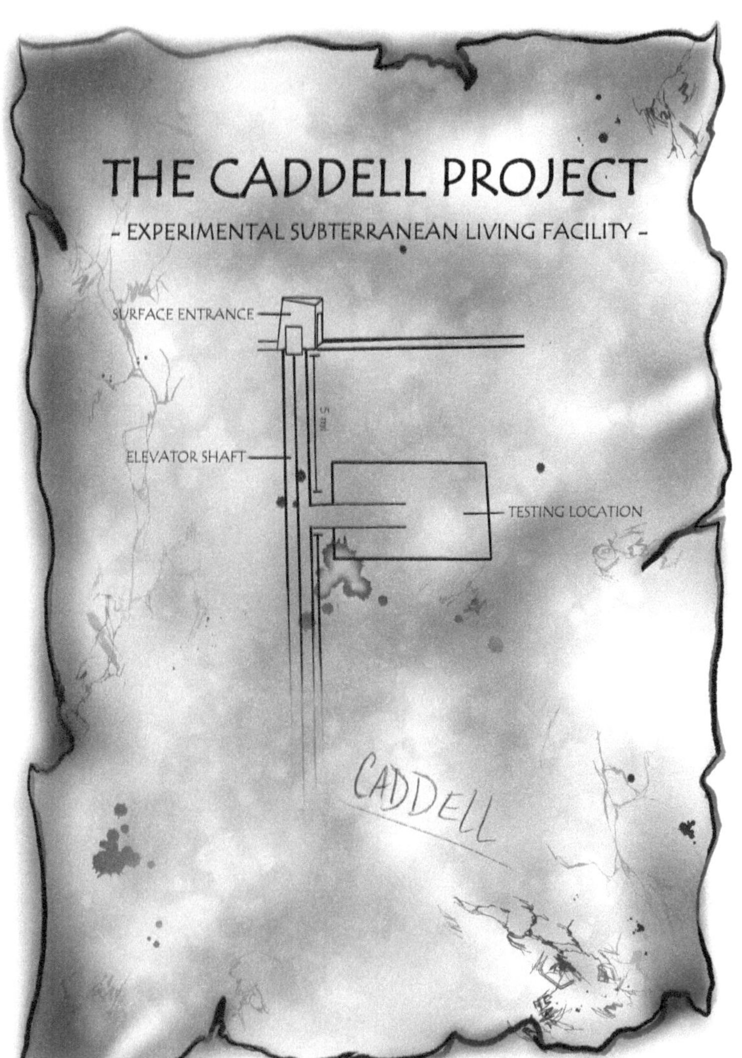
THE CADDELL PROJECT
- EXPERIMENTAL SUBTERRANEAN LIVING FACILITY -
SURFACE ENTRANCE
ELEVATOR SHAFT
TESTING LOCATION
CADDELL

The date scheduled for transport of the final testing group, The Selected #008, is set for 11.23.2052. On this day, residents of the project will be removed from the Testing Location and will be taken to the permanent living facility of Caddell. Once the final group has been safely relocated, the Testing Location self-destruction will take place. Project inhabitants will remain enclosed in Caddell, having no further knowledge of surface condition or any other world left beyond that in which they are contained in.

About the Author

E.M. Daniels is from central Florida, where she lived with her family before moving further north in the state to pursue her education and start a life together with her husband. When she isn't writing, she enjoys being involved in agriculture, drawing (mainly using charcoal), and going to the movie theater. She also loves spending time with her dog "Jess" in which she named after a very special character she enjoyed creating and writing about. *The Caddell Project* is her first novel, though she plans to continue writing and already has several more stories in the works.

www.ingramcontent.com/pod-product-compliance
Lightning Source LLC
Chambersburg PA
CBHW030610310726
48979CB00003B/652

9798991606417